# HIRED:
# SASSY
# ASSISTANT

# HIRED: SASSY ASSISTANT

BY

NINA HARRINGTON

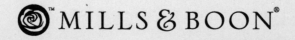

First published in Great Britain 2009
Large Print edition 2010
Harlequin Mills & Boon Limited,
Eton House, 18-24 Paradise Road,
Richmond, Surrey TW9 1SR

© Nina Harrington 2009

ISBN: 978 0 263 21211 2

Harlequin Mills & Boon policy is to use papers that are
natural, renewable and recyclable products and made
from wood grown in sustainable forests. The logging and
manufacturing process conform to the legal environmental
regulations of the country of origin.

Printed and bound in Great Britain
by CPI Antony Rowe, Chippenham, Wiltshire

To Stephen. For everything.

# CHAPTER ONE

IT WASN'T every day of the week that you saw a librarian carrying a package on her head that looked bigger than she was, struggling to get off a London tube train at eleven o'clock in the morning.

Especially when that librarian had sun-streaked blond corkscrew hair that fell around her shoulders in long, wavy tendrils.

As he stepped out onto the platform, Kyle Munroe glanced back to the next carriage just in time to see the librarian stretch up on tiptoes, lift the wide bag over the heads of her fellow passengers, then thrust it forward to use as a wedge through the crush of travellers rushing past her to board the train. They had little regard for anyone who might dare to get in their way.

Seconds before the train door beeped closed behind her, the blonde had to practically jump onto the platform, before snatching the package out of the jaws of the sliding doors with such force that she almost fell backwards as the tube sped away.

The librarian tried to restore her dignity by tugging the jacket of her dove-grey skirt suit a little lower, and lifting her cute, small nose a little higher, before hoisting the straps of what looked like an artist's portfolio case over her neck and shoulder. Only the bag was still dragging on the floor, so she forgot the straps and went for Plan B. This involved holding the edges of the case with her fingertips, arms at full stretch, while trying to hitch the wide strap around her neck with one shoulderblade and her chin.

After two trial steps in amazingly rickety-looking heels, she strode forward, the portfolio flapping against her chest, head high, eyes set on her goal— the escalator. Only Plan B let her down, and she was reduced to sliding, dragging and cajoling her oversized package towards the escalator.

Perhaps she was actually a schoolteacher, and

any second now she would tell the unruly portfolio to go and sit in the naughty corner?

Nope—she was definitely a librarian. The only woman he had ever seen wearing that kind of dull grey skirt suit by choice had been the technical librarian at his medical school. That particular lady could dance a mean mambo, and was a world expert on parasitic diseases, but she still chose those hideous suits!

Then again, she had never, ever worn dove-grey mules below legs like the ones trying to walk ahead of him at that minute—the kind of legs that forced the first smile of the day from his lips.

So what if he was a leg man and proud of it?

This was turning out to be the high point of a journey that had started in squalor and sunshine a long way from London. Three hours across the mountains in a bone-shaking Jeep with bald tyres had been followed by a very long flight in economy class, surrounded by wonderful but exhausted screaming kids. Coming up with games and toys to amuse them had been fun—for the first couple of hours.

It had been a long day, and his body clock was starting to kick in. Perhaps it was time to show his appreciation for the lady who had finally given him something to smile about?

With his long athletic legs, and her shorter, high-heeled ones, it only took Kyle a few steps to catch up with her.

'Do you need any help with that?' he asked, trying to sound casual and non-threatening.

The librarian didn't break stride as she took a sideways glance at his six feet one of athletic hunkiness—or at least that was how the TV company liked to describe him. From the stunned look in her pale blue eyes, she had decided that he was clearly not to be trusted.

He tried to act casual by running a few fingers through his shaggy, dark brown, now mostly dust encrusted hair. Hmm. Not his best look. Perhaps he should have made the time to take a shower and change his clothes at the airport?

'I'm fine, but thank you for offering.'

Except the words were barely out of her mouth before the portfolio slid off her shoulder and Kyle had to reach forward to stop it from being trampled underfoot by the crush of passengers trying to cram onto the escalator.

As they were swept along in the rush, the librarian took a sharp intake of breath and clutched onto the handrail. Her other hand was pressed to her throat, where a red welt showed that the weight of the bag was very far from being fine.

'It's okay—I've got it,' Kyle reassured her. 'Maybe I could carry it as far as the barrier? How about that?'

'Okay, just to the barrier.'

She half turned around to face him, and he was struck by her closed-mouth smile. His medical head noticed immediately that her right eye was flecked with deeper shades of blue than the other. Whatever she saw in his face he could only guess, but the half-smile creased the corner of a wide, plump mouth set in creamy skin sprinkled with freckles over her nose and cheeks. Like cinnamon powder on whipped cream.

Freckles. Why did she have to have freckles? He almost groaned. *Doomed.*

'I see that you've flown from Delhi. That's a long flight. Been there on holiday?' she asked, her dainty head tipped slightly in the cutest, loveliest, most freckly pose.

Drat! The airline tags were still attached to his old rucksack!

'Just passing through,' he replied, trying to sound flippant, before nodding over her shoulder. 'Here we go.'

The librarian suddenly realised that they were at the top of the escalator, and whipped around so that she could step to one side and stay within touching distance of her precious package.

He took a firmer grip on what felt like a thin wooden frame—not heavy, but an awkward size and shape—and casually swept the handles over one shoulder.

'What sort of picture is this?' he asked as he fumbled for his ticket, half expecting to hear that it was some Old Master bound for restoration by learned scholars in an ancient London guild.

'Orchids. Yellow orchids, to be exact.' She paused and nodded. 'I'm sure I can manage from here. It's only a short bus ride to the South Bank. Sorry to have been such a nuisance.'

'No apology necessary.' Kyle was just about to pass the portfolio over when he paused. 'Did you say the South Bank? That's where I'm headed. Why don't we share a cab?' He hoisted the bag a little higher. 'The bus could be a problem.'

Even though she had been the first to mention her destination, she hesitated, clearly weighing up the benefits of getting there in one piece against the danger from a scruffy potential stalker and orchid-picture thief. Kyle stared at her silence as she bit her lower lip before going for it.

'Um, okay. Yes, that would be great. Thank you. Normally I would walk along the Embankment—but not in these shoes, carrying that. And I am rather late.'

'Me too. Shall we risk it?'

That seemed to stun her for a few seconds, but with a gentle nod, the blonde climbed the steps out of the station. The crush of other pedestrians and the awkward shape of the portfolio conspired together to thwart most of Kyle's view of the spectacular legs in action on the stairs, but the little he did see was well worth the effort.

It took only minutes to clamber out into the noise and chaos of the city street. After eighteen months in the mountains he had forgotten what a physical assault on the senses it all was, and the girl in the grey suit had hailed a black cab before he'd pulled himself together.

Kyle made a point of swinging the package onto the backseat, then holding open the door for her before jumping in himself with his rucksack.

While he knew as much about London art galleries as she probably did about yaks, the name the librarian gave to their driver sounded familiar enough for him to be impressed.

As their cab took off into the traffic she collapsed back against her seat and slowly exhaled, her arm wrapped protectively around the edge of the portfolio.

'Are there a lot of career opportunities for art couriers these days?'

She looked across at him as though she had almost forgotten that he was there.

'Oh, this is only a sideline,' she replied in a matter-of-fact voice. 'My real job is in art forgery. That's where the real money is.' She leant closer and whispered, 'But I'm relying on you to keep my secret to yourself.'

'My lips are sealed. Best of luck in prison.'

The blue eyes crinkled up into a smile as she took in his filthy jacket, two-day stubble and the trousers that had last seen water two weeks earlier after an emergency Caesarean section on a riverbank.

'Passing through Delhi? That sounds like a lot of fun. Is it still warm and sunny there?' she asked in a light-hearted voice.

'Very,' he replied with a sigh. 'At this time of year they're getting ready for Diwali—the festival of lights. I'm sorry I'm missing that! It's a fantastic city. Do you know it?'

'Not personally,' she replied, then gave him a wistful smile. 'But people have told me about the wonderful colours and the atmosphere. I've always wanted to go there. Maybe one day,' she added, shrugging her shoulders. Then the blonde gestured towards his jacket with her head. 'I can see that you've spent time in the mountains. Let me guess. Have you been climbing or hiking?'

Wow. She really was observant. It was a pity that the truth was far too complicated, because ideally he would have loved to find the time to do precisely those things. But he had never got the chance.

'Not even close. What makes you think that I've been in the mountains?'

She grinned back before replying. 'I noticed that you're wearing a white Buddhist scarf, and you have Hindi graffiti scribbled on your arm.'

Kyle stared down at the plaster cast encasing his left wrist, which was completely covered with colourful messages. Um. Perhaps some of them were a bit crude.

'You can read Nepali?' he asked, with genuine admiration in his voice.

'No, but I do recognise the Hindi characters,' she held up one hand, palm forward. 'And I don't need a translation, if it's all the same to you.'

'Probably just as well. I'm Kyle, by the way.'

He reached forward with his right hand, and she glanced at it for a second before giving it a firm, quick shake with small, thin, cool fingers. His rough fingertips rasped in contact with her delicate skin. Perhaps that was why she pulled back immediately, as the cab slowed for some lights, and started scrabbling about in her messenger bag?

'I could give you my name,' she replied, 'but I am on a very important mission where secrecy is vital. That sort of personal information is strictly on a need-to-know basis. This should cover my share of the cab fare.'

Kyle looked at the pile of coins she had passed him in bewilderment, and wondered if cab fares had increased at the same rate as female sass since he had been away.

'A mission at the art gallery? Ah. Of course. The old forgery trade.' He tapped his nose twice. 'Your secret is safe. What are you running late for?'

'I have to drop this off and then make a twelve-o'clock appointment. I'm cutting it fine.' She glanced at her watch, and noticed that he was not wearing one. 'How about you, Kyle? What are you late for? Oh, sorry—another time. This is the gallery.'

She flashed a beaming smile in his direction as the cab slowed in front of an elegant glass-fronted building. 'It's been a pleasure, and thanks again. I hope I haven't delayed you too much.'

'Wait,' Kyle replied, pushing the bag towards her. 'One question. Please? I have to know. Are you a librarian, by any chance?'

She stopped trying to drag the portfolio over her shoulder and looked at him wide-eyed for a second, before breaking into the kind of warm smile that stopped traffic and turned curly haired, blond librarians into supermodels.

'Not even close.' And with that she closed the cab door and gave him a regal wave, before striding away without looking back.

Twenty minutes later Lulu Hamilton sauntered down the wide South Bank pavement as best as she could in her godmother Emma's dove-grey mules, and revelled in the sights and smells of the crisp, late-October day.

As a beam of bright sunshine broke through the clouds she dropped her head back and closed her eyes to enjoy the moment.

Not bad, girl. Not bad at all. She had reached the gallery right on time. The job was done. It had meant sharing a taxi with a cheeky tourist with a killer smile, but for once her risky decision had paid off and she had delivered her painting in one piece.

The yellow orchid acrylic was destined for a luxury boutique in the city. The gallery was delighted, the client was thrilled, and best of all, she had been paid a bonus for delivering the piece in time for their grand opening. If she kept to a tight budget, the cheque in her pocket would see her through the first few months of art college. Her dream had just come one step closer.

She inhaled deeply, soaking in the sights and smells of the city. Ten years ago she had been a student here, before she'd left university to take care of her father after her mother was killed. She rarely came back. It was too painful to think about what could have been.

Not any longer. That was then and this was now.

For the first time in many years she was finally moving forward with her life and putting the past behind her. So what if it was a baby step, and she had a few steep hills head? Mountains, even? She was moving forward and she was doing it through her own hard work.

One thing was certain. She had forgotten how crowded the city was—and how noisy. The traffic din was worse than ever. The cacophony of mixed fragments of sound from buses, taxicabs, cars and people seemed to collide inside her brain.

Well, that was something she could control!

In one smooth, well-practised motion, her finger-tips smoothed her shoulder-length hair down over her left ear and, oblivious to anyone else, she turned off the small digital hearing aid fitted behind it.

That was better. Much better.

Brightly coloured leaves in amazing shades of scarlet and russet, from the maples and London plane trees which lined the Embankment, blew against her legs in the fresh breeze from the Thames.

She loved autumn—it had always been her favourite season.

She couldn't imagine living in a tropical climate. Not when nature put on this glorious free display for people to enjoy.

The last few months had been tough, but the painting had been finished on time and it was as good as anything she had ever done. Perhaps her friends back home in Kingsmede were right, and she should take some time out to enjoy herself for a change and smell the rosebuds?

A half-smile creased her face as she glanced at her fellow pedestrians, crowding the pavement. Most of them either had their noses pressed into the pages of a tourist guidebook, or were chatting away on cellphone headsets while keying something desperately important into a personal organiser.

With a brisk shake of her head, Lulu twirled around a cluster of teenage tourists, then swallowed down hard as her gaze fixed straight ahead on the impressive entrance to the stylish media company offices, where the book launch event was being held.

It was still a total mystery why Mike Baxter had invited her to this book launch at all. Of course she had been thrilled to hear that he had been promoted to Clinical Director at the medical foundation where her mother had worked for the last eight years of her life, but his letter had certainly been intriguing.

They had kept in contact, but this was the first time that Mike had invited her to a press conference—so that he could talk to her about an 'exciting opportunity' over lunch. Mike was one of the few people who knew about her partial hearing, and that crowded public events were not her favourite places.

After almost twenty-nine years on the planet, the words *exciting* combined with *opportunity* usually meant a lot of work for her with all the kudos going to other people. Except that Mike had made it clear that this was going to be a great way to raise money for her local hospice, where her father had spent the last few weeks of his life.

And for that she was willing to face a crowded room full of chattering people, most of whom she would not be able to hear, and questions about a woman who had been dead ten years and yet still managed to control her life.

Ruth Taylor Hamilton. Her celebrity mother. The famous pioneering surgeon.

The very last person she wanted to talk about. Ever.

Kyle Monroe stared out of the office window at the overcast sky of central London in October. It was hard to believe that only eighteen hours earlier he had been trekking through sunlit forests in the foothills of Nepal.

His eyes felt heavy, gritty, ready to close, but just as Kyle's head fell back onto the sofa cushion, Mike Baxter finished the call on his mobile phone.

'They're ready and waiting for us. Did you get any sleep at all on the flight? Eight hours, wasn't it? Nine?'

'More like twelve—and, no, not much. The flight was packed.' Kyle yawned. 'You forget what airport crowds are like. The noise. The stress. The smell.' He raised his right arm and sniffed. 'Speaking of which, is there any chance I can get a shave and a shower? I think I startled a pretty girl on the tube this morning.'

'Nope,' Mike replied. 'We're already late. Besides, you have the perfect image—the media company have been working on it. "Dedicated medic flies in straight from the clinic, still in his working clothes." Natural grunge. The press will love it.'

Then he looked more closely at something on Kyle's clothes and recoiled back. 'Are those bloodstains on your trousers?'

Kyle reached down and casually pulled up one leg of his cargo trousers, revealing a surprisingly white, muscular hairy leg. 'Ketchup. Or chilli sauce.' He nodded. 'Probably chilli sauce. The blood is on my jacket. Sorry about that, but we had to use the last of the soap powder to clean the sheets. TB clinics wash a lot of laundry.'

Mike gave a quick nod. 'No problem. Now, what's the story with your wrist?'

Kyle waggled the crusty filthy plaster cast which encased his lower left arm.

'Clean break. My own fault for sticking my arm out when I fell off a rope ladder. It was the only way across the ravine. I tried to do some sort of judo break-fall. And it worked. It broke. No problem.' He shrugged. 'The cast is coming off next week.'

'Any photographs from this ravine?' Mike asked, suddenly interested. 'They could always come in useful for the next book!'

'Next one?' Kyle laughed. 'I barely had time to write this one, Mike! Keep an online diary of your climbing and your medical life, you said. Take a few photos every now and then and post them on your blog, you said. Now look where it's got me!'

Mike lifted up his laptop computer and waved it in Kyle's direction. 'Over ten thousand hits a day. Online diaries are big business now. The income from your first book will pay for the entire Nepalese mission for the next few years. It's the best investment the foundation has ever seen!'

Mike came around to perch on the end of his desk.

'Look, Kyle, I need to talk business for a minute—so you can start groaning now. The way I see it, you're going to be out of action for at least another month. Am I right? Your wrist has not healed properly, and you need to get what's left of that chest infection out of your body.' Mike paused long enough to rub his hands along the edge of his desk in a nervous gesture. 'And then there is the real reason that I pulled you back from the mission. I know you don't want to talk about it, but from what your half-brother told me your family problems might take longer to resolve than you think.'

He was met with a shrug. 'That's not why I'm here,' Kyle replied. 'The rabies programme is behind schedule. That has to come before my personal issues. We need those vaccines, and we need them today. My job is to raise the money to make that happen.'

Mike looked hard into Kyle's face. 'Which is why I've been working with the TV company to pull together an amazing deal for your rabies project.'

Kyle sat up, his brows pulled together in concentration. 'What kind of deal? I don't know what else I can say about Nepal.'

Mike nodded. 'You're right. The film crew has already been to Nepal, and they have everything they need.' He paused and sat back. 'You might not have realised it, but you talked a lot over the past year about your very first mission. You went straight out of medical school into a war zone in Africa. I think you actually came out and stated on camera that it was a life-changing experience.'

There were a few seconds of silence before Kyle responded in a low voice, 'It *was* life-changing. For all of us.'

'That's why the producer wants to make a documentary about your first mission to Uganda. The problems you faced. How it inspired you. The film will probably be shown around March next year. If you could write a book about your diary from those days, and if it can be ready at the same time, it could be a top-seller.'

'Uganda?' Kyle breathed. 'That was ten long years ago, Mike, and I'm not sure I want to go back there. Even on paper.'

'They've offered to double your last advance to make it happen.'

There was another silence before Kyle coughed. 'Did you say double?'

Mike simply nodded. 'If you can force yourself to sit in one place long enough to finish this second book, you can be back in Nepal before the winter sets in—with enough cash to pay the drugs bill for at least the next five years, including all of the vaccines you've asked for.'

Kyle sat back and blew out hard, before shaking his head in resignation.

'You know me too well. When do they need the finished book?'

'The first draft is due in a month. But I know you like challenges,' Mike replied casually as he shrugged into his jacket.

'A month? You know what I'm like with paper-work! I haven't typed anything longer than a few paragraphs for my blog since university!'

Mike didn't even try to argue. 'We have a few suggestions on how we can help you with that—but later. Ready to rock and roll? All you have to do is enjoy the free beer, eat the snacks—and smile. Big smile. Use your charm. Think of the vaccines your book is going to bring into that clinic of yours. Leave me to make sure the press go away happy.'

Kyle grinned back. 'Free beer? What kind of beer?'

# CHAPTER TWO

'DR BAXTER should be arriving with Dr Munroe any time now, Miss Hamilton,' the excited little secretary said, almost rocking in her seat behind the wide curved reception desk.

Lulu locked her smile firmly into place before replying in a sweet voice, 'You did say the same thing forty minutes ago, Marta. Are you sure this time?'

'Dr Munroe's flight was delayed, but they are on their way.' The young girl swallowed, smoothed down her mini skirt and gazed in wonder at the stack of books on the desk. 'Isn't Dr Munroe the dreamiest? Perhaps I could persuade him to sign my book for me?'

Each chair in the stylish reception area carried

a copy of a paperback book with the words *Medicine Man* in large dark letters.

But it was the stunning cover that was designed to captivate and enthral.

It was an amateur photograph of a bearded young man, in brightly coloured clothing and large dark goggles, standing in deep white snow, with high mountain peaks behind him, reflecting bright sunshine. Buddhist prayer flags fluttered in the breeze above his head against a cobalt-blue sky.

He was grinning widely for the camera, clearly full of life.

According to the press release tucked into each book, K. B. Munroe was a British doctor doing pioneering work on disease control in the High Himalaya of Nepal.

From what Lulu could see, the photograph might just as well have been from a fashion shoot for an adventure sports magazine. Only there was something extra-special in the single image that shone from the man himself. She could not see his face behind the beard and the goggles, yet his energy leapt from the photograph. A life-force so powerful it was practically hypnotic.

The photograph was clearly of some sort of strange mythical creature—because this medic was one broad-shouldered, tanned, handsome and unshaven hunk. All in all, a tousle-haired, square-jawed dream of an emergency doctor and moun-taineer. Beyond rugged. Relaxed. In total control. Captured for ever in a moment. Frozen in time.

The creature in that photo could have been a film actor playing the part. Maybe that was it? Maybe the real Dr Munroe was a wizened and cynical hard nut, still tramping through the ice and snow in Nepal, and the publisher had taken the easy way out with a gorgeous action-hero actor to play the role?

She smiled to herself. Doctors like K. B. Munroe did wonderful work in hard conditions. They deserved every scrap of praise and recognition. But she knew better than most people that the reality of that life was anything but attractive. Nobody should have to make those kinds of sacrifices.

As she picked up the book and looked more closely at the heroic figure on the cover, she could not help but wonder if this man had a wife and children back home. How did *they* feel when he left them for the mountains? Not knowing if they would ever see him again?

A cold shiver ran down her spine and she almost dropped the book back onto the chair. Too many memories. Too many ghosts.

Suddenly aware that Marta was still waiting for some kind of response from her, Lulu held back on her honest opinion and managed a polite, 'Oh, yes, he certainly is something. Do you think there is time for another tea before they get here?'

'Tea? Right, sure. Rush job. Don't want to miss him,' the receptionist blurted out, and scurried off in the direction from where the previous two cups of tea had come in the forty minutes Lulu had been waiting, at about twice the speed she had before.

Lulu stood up and slipped the glossy style magazine back onto the flimsy black-and-red Japanese lacquer table beside a massive scarlet leather sofa.

Everything in the reception area shouted expensive, stylish—and in Lulu's eyes would be as long-lasting as the display of tall living white orchids which had been placed in the best position to catch the October blast from the Thames that blew in every time the doors slid open on the London street. Disaster!

She sauntered over as gracefully as she could in her borrowed shoes and fitted skirt, and checked the blossoms and leaves of the stunning blooms. If only the orchids in her conservatory back in Kingsmede were as lovely as these. They would look wonderful painted in a blue-and-white Delft porcelain bowl. Or perhaps against a backdrop of delicate foliage and lavender?

Lulu was so engrossed that she jumped back in surprise as she was suddenly jolted into the real world when the main street door was flung wide-open, sending it crashing against a chair. She turned back just in time to see a tall, gangly bundle of momentum and a flash of filthy stained khaki stride away from her towards the reception desk.

He had come 'In' through the 'Out' door.

A dark green, stained and heavy-looking military rucksack missed a stunned media company executive in a suit by inches as it swung out from one shoulder to the other. Judging from his back view, Lulu guessed this was a journalist who had just been involved in a street fight.

His stride was confident, powerful and energetic. Strong. Someone who knew exactly what he was doing and where he was going in life.

He had probably not even noticed her existence. Typical. Nothing new there.

She was glad when he pushed his way past the red sofa and dropped his heavy bag before the desk.

After looking from side to side a couple of times, he half turned, caught sight of her, and turned on a killer smile.

She had seen his back view a few minutes earlier.

Now Lulu got the full glory. And her mouth dropped open in surprise.

This man smiling across at her was the same tourist who had helped to carry her picture and shared her black cab not two hours earlier.

No doubt about it.

It was the crown prince of grunge.

As he strolled towards her, slowly this time, the

confident swagger of his hips completing his hypnotic charm, Lulu could not look away from his face. In an instant she made the connection with the cover image on the book next to her.

*He* was *Medicine Man*.

K. B. Munroe. Kyle Munroe.

In one smooth movement she lifted her head, straightened her back and inhaled a fortifying breath. So what if she had always been attracted to the athletic type of man? She could handle this.

The adrenaline junkie sidled up to her with his best charm offensive. Lulu decided to take the initiative this time and stretched out her right hand. 'Hello, again. This is a pleasant surprise.'

Kyle stepped closer, but instead of releasing her fingers he raised the back of her hand to his lips, trying to avoid his sharp stubbly chin.

'The pleasure is all mine. It would seem that fate has had the good taste to put us in the same place at the same time. I had no idea that TV companies needed librarians.'

He slowly turned his head from side to side, looking around the echoing reception area before whispering, 'Or specialist art dealers…' And he gave her the kind of twinkly-eyed smile guaranteed to make any girl's heart beat a little faster.

And it was certainly effective! Lulu dragged her eyes away from his face as she slowly retrieved her fingers and casually picked up one of the books from the coffee table before waving it in his direction. 'Well, I wouldn't know about that. Seeing as I'm not a librarian. Dr Munroe, I presume?'

He shrugged. 'That's me. Did you make it to the gallery in time?' Then he leant closer. 'I don't know how undercover art forgers work, but if you have any influence around here at all, I shall have to throw myself on your mercy. If you can point me in the direction of a cold beer, I shall be your slave for a week.'

'Only a week?' Then her smile widened. 'I was right on time, so thanks for your help. You'll find the buffet and an open bar just through there— although…' She glanced down at her watch. 'You are running a little late. The presentation was due to start ten minutes ago.'

'No problem at all. You would be amazed at

what I can achieve in ten minutes. Now, please allow me to do something to show my gratitude.'

He moved closer and leant his head towards her, and for a horrible, exciting, heart-thumping moment she thought he might kiss her. But as she leant back he simply laughed and gestured to the paperback with his photo on the cover, which she was still clutching to her side.

'Would you like me to sign your book for you?'

Lulu grinned back in relief, and possibly a touch of regret. He was good at this.

'Yes, please. If you could address it to my friend, Marta, that would be great.'

'No problem at all. I hope your *friend* likes it. Marta.'

Kyle squiggled a signature, then raised his eyebrows a few times before giving her another very saucy wink and a dazzling flash of white teeth, sweeping up his rucksack and striding over to the side entrance—just as Marta practically jogged up to the reception desk, splattering tea on the glossy black floor tiles before turning around to glare at Lulu in disgust.

Lulu was just about to explain when Marta stepped away to one side. 'Dr Baxter. You are running terribly late. Miss Hamilton has been waiting for ages!'

The next thing Lulu knew she was being crushed into a hug by a huge bear of a man with grey hair and wearing a smart business suit.

'Lulu—I am so sorry. But the Delhi flight was almost two hours late and the PR crew have tried to drink the bar dry. Let's get the launch out of the way so we can talk properly. Oh. Is that for me? Thanks, Marta. You're a star.'

And in one action Mike swallowed down what was left of Lulu's cup of tea, grabbed her arm, and almost dragged her towards the conference room, talking fast enough to stop her getting a word in edgeways. 'You look amazing, by the way. How have you been keeping?'

Five minutes of blurred, frantic activity later, Lulu was sitting in the second row in the conference room, watching Mike Baxter arrange his notes on the lectern. She was not entirely sure how she had come to be sitting there, in a crush of photographers, media company executives and journalists who all seemed to be talking non-stop.

She was starting to regret turning her hearing aid back on.

Mike waited patiently for the chatter and clatter to subside, before speaking into the microphone.

'Ladies and gentlemen. If you could take your seats? Thank you. My name is Mike Baxter, and it is my pleasure to welcome you all here today in my capacity as Medical Director of the Medical Foundation for Humanitarian Aid.'

He paused as the press settled into their chairs. 'As some of you will know, twelve months ago the foundation was asked by one of the largest television and multimedia companies in the western world to nominate three unique medical professionals working in hazardous conditions around the world who would be willing to be filmed as part of a TV series. Each mission would receive a charitable donation worth fifty thousand pounds. When that film was broadcast, earlier in the year, it soon became clear that one doctor in particular had touched the hearts of the viewers. Dr Kyle Munroe.'

Mike paused and looked around the room, making sure that he had the full attention of the audience before making his announcement.

'Ladies and gentlemen. What happened next has surprised us all. The programme made a bestseller of *Medicine Man* by Kyle Munroe. This book began as an online diary created during his first year spent working in the high Himalaya of Nepal. The diary is absolutely gripping from beginning to end, and has never been out of the top-ten list. I am pleased to announce that today marks publication of the paperback edition of the book, with a new introduction by the author.'

Mike Baxter glanced to someone at the back of the hall and nodded.

'I am delighted to tell you that the man himself has literally just got off a plane from Delhi, after travelling by foot, Jeep, and two international flights to be with us today. Ladies and gentlemen—Dr Kyle Balfour Munroe!'

The sandwich-chomping journo sitting in front

of her, and everyone else around her, stood up to applaud, blocking Lulu's view and forcing her to step out into the side aisle just as Kyle stepped onto the podium from her side of the room. He was holding a pint glass of beer in his right hand, while trying to salute Mike with his plaster cast.

Only now he was wearing spectacles with thin metal rims, which instantly turned him into a younger and jaw-droppingly handsome version of Indiana Jones.

It might be sneaky, but it certainly was effective, and Lulu could not take her eyes from Kyle's face as he casually passed the beer glass to Mike Baxter so that he could raise up a copy of the paperback with his good right hand.

Turning to the microphone, Kyle cracked a beaming smile, displaying brilliant white teeth against his deeply tanned skin. She could see the corners of his mouth wrinkle up with the grin, the tiny pale lines radiating out from his full lips. The thin spectacles seemed to highlight his deep chocolate caramel hair and hazel green eyes. The kind of caramel a girl could savour and linger over for as long as possible, desperate to prolong the delicious pleasure.

Every eye in the room was focused on him long before he spoke.

'I am delighted to be here today to launch the new edition of *Medicine Man*. Every single person who bought the book has already made a huge difference to the lives of the people I work with on a daily basis. People who depend on you for the health of themselves and their families. On their behalf, I thank you all.'

And then he did it. He used the knuckle of his forefinger to just touch the end of his nose and push his spectacles higher. As though to conceal a glistening tear.

As the audience took a breath, Lulu stretched her head up over the reporter's heads as the scruffy Adonis stuffed the book casually into the front pocket of his cargo pants, retrieved his beer with a nod of thanks, and raised the glass to salute the rows of press and photographers, his face barely visible behind the flashguns and microphones.

Then he was swallowed up in the crush.

Mike paused for a few minutes for photographs, before valiantly making his way through the rugby scrum of press already six deep around the podium, each desperate to capture the human interest cover story for the next day. A few seconds later he came to stand next to Lulu. He didn't even try to lower his voice as they stood watching the scene.

'I know he's a bit rough around the edges, but that boy has raised more money for the foundation in the last twelve months than in the previous five years put together. We want Kyle to write a second book, about the time he spent with your mother in Uganda, and the foundation needs *you* to help him do that. What do you say?'

'Mike Baxter, you have an awful lot of explaining to do. And I think you had better start right now. You *know* how I feel about that subject. Please tell me why I shouldn't get the next train back to Kingsmede right now?'

'Well, I might do if you stopped pacing for

five minutes. Did you read the dedication in Kyle's book?'

Lulu turned to face her mother's old friend and planted her hands on her hips before giving him a disbelieving look. 'That would be difficult, since I had never even heard of Kyle Munroe until today.'

Mike sighed and flicked to a specific page before passing the paperback over to her.

'Perhaps you should finally get around to buying a television some time soon? Anyhow, you might want to see this before we go any further.'

Lulu breathed out in exasperation and glared at him before accepting the open book and glancing down at the page.

*This diary is humbly dedicated to Dr Ruth Taylor Hamilton, who started me on this crazy journey in the first place. The sacrifice and untimely death of this remarkable surgeon taught me what it means to be an emergency medic. Maybe one day I can come close to being that good. Thank you, Stitch. I owe you one.*

Her balloon of annoyance popped into ragged shreds of flimsy plastic. Lulu sat down on the hard chair in the now-empty conference room and read it again. 'Oh.'

As she passed the book back to Mike, she felt sure that the thundering of her heart was loud enough for him to hear.

When she did force the air back into her frozen lungs, she saw that his eyes were still looking into her face. Intense.

Unlike the squeaky voice that emerged when she did try to speak through a bone-dry throat. 'Did they work together?'

'Uganda.'

She closed her eyes and tried to block out the horror of what that experience must have been like. 'Her last mission.'

'There's more. Kyle needs every penny we can raise to fund the infectious disease campaign. The TV company want to film a documentary about the Uganda mission and publish Kyle's diaries from that time. He needs help to make that happen.'

Lulu stood up and paced across to the podium

in silence, before turning back to face her mother's friend. 'You don't need me! You need a professional editor.'

He nodded. 'Yes, I could hire someone. But they couldn't help Kyle like you can.'

There was something in his voice which caught Lulu's attention. 'What do you mean, like I can?'

'Do you remember the last time I came to Kingsmede? When Tom was still at home?'

'Of course.' She smiled back. 'Dad loved seeing you.'

'Tom made a point of showing me the work you had both done to organise the boxes of your mother's personal items we shipped back from Africa. You did a great job with sorting that lot out. I know he was proud of you for sticking with it and seeing it through. It must have been hard.'

Lulu swallowed down hard. 'Very. Where are you going with this, Mike?'

He lifted his head and looked her straight in the eyes.

'Kyle needs the letters and diaries your mother wrote from Uganda to help him write his book.'

Her face paled, and she had opened her mouth to tell him precisely what he could do with that idea when he raised one hand, palm up.

'Before you say no, please let me explain.'

Mike dropped his hands to his knees and spoke in a low voice.

'Kyle has already mentioned in interviews that Ruth Taylor Hamilton was the reason he got into emergency medicine. The media company have been inundated with requests for more information about this mysterious person, and they came to me.'

He waved his arms dramatically in the air while shrugging his shoulders. 'Things took off from there. I mentioned that your dad had collected together Ruth's letters and diaries from her time in Uganda, and the next thing I knew the publishing director wanted to know how soon they could have Kyle's manuscript about the time he spent in Africa! It's crazy, but they are serious. They want him to talk about Ruth and her work and how it inspired him.'

Lulu sucked in a breath and swallowed down

the wave of nausea that swept through her. 'What? Not now!'

'Why not now? This is the perfect time! Kyle has already done the promotion work in advance! You couldn't ask for better publicity.'

'I think you might be forgetting something. My father and I didn't finish the work, and it would take months to pull everything together even if I wanted to do it. Which I don't.'

Mike held out a piece of paper with numbers written on it, and stretched it out in front of her eyes with a thumb and forefinger at each end.

Lulu inhaled sharply. Her eyes refused to take in the figure with several zeros at the end of it, and her brain stopped working as she blinked several times in rapid succession.

'They want this to be a very personal record. That was what made Kyle's first book so special. This would be one single payment. A consultancy fee, if you like.'

Lulu sat back in the chair and looked at the numbers again. 'You're serious about this, aren't you?'

'Very. The foundation gets a generous charitable donation, plus income from the film and the book, and this money is yours to do with as you will. And don't tell me that you couldn't put it to good use.'

Her brain went into overdrive.

Art college? Paid for by profits from her mother's sweat and ultimate self-sacrifice? No. She could never do that. However…

Lulu groaned out loud. 'Dad would want any money from the book to go to the hospice. It desperately needs a respite centre.'

'The hospice where Tom died?'

She nodded. 'They were brilliant. This money would probably pay for most of the work. I certainly don't have any spare cash to give them.'

Then the true impact of what he was talking about hit home.

'Wait a moment, Mike. This is going too fast. I need to think about this a lot more before agreeing to anything. You know that she wrote a letter home almost every week? I would have to read through all of her papers before Kyle could look at them. That could take weeks.' She sat back and shook her head. 'I'm not sure this could work. I'm only a bookkeeper and part-time artist from Kingsmede.'

'You're Ruth and Tom's daughter. They were two of the most extraordinary people I have ever met. And so are you. You can handle it. Besides, I have an idea about how I can help you pull it off.'

'I don't like the sound of that, but go on.'

Mike smiled and picked up Kyle's book. 'Kyle is a wonderful doctor and a good man, but he'd be the first to admit that paperwork is not one of his priorities. I paid two temporary secretaries to pull together his blog and the background material for this book, and they struggled with the technical details. The second book is going to be harder. He has already told me that his notes and diaries are scrappy at best. He needs help from someone who has done this before and can work with a field medic—otherwise he won't stand a chance of doing justice to the amazing work they did ten years ago.'

Lulu inhaled sharply. 'You can't be serious.'

'It's not as bad as it sounds. Kyle was only in Uganda for nine months. What he needs is help to put his boxes of personal notes into some sort of order so he can turn around the second book before he goes back to Nepal.'

'Just putting everything in order from those nine months? That's it? Simple admin and typing?'

'That's it. Kyle's notes will form the core of the book. Your mum's records covering those nine months will add the next level of detail.'

'And what does Boy Wonder think of this plan?'

'He doesn't know a thing. I thought I had better discuss it with you first. Why don't we go and break the happy news over lunch?'

'So he *could* say no?'

Mike looked at her over the top of his spectacles in disbelief. 'He could. But then he would miss the chance of spending time with a lovely young lady such as yourself. Most unlikely.' He smiled as she groaned in horror, and linked her arm over his. 'Can I tempt you with food and wine, madam?'

'Lead the way. I feel like I'm going to need it.'

# CHAPTER THREE

LULU sat alone in the far corner of the bar and watched as the media executives circled around Kyle like vultures flying above a prime piece of food.

Mike Baxter had been instantly snatched away by medical journalists, all desperate for an exclusive interview with the bestselling author and media star who was currently holding court from his bar stool. Kyle had made a joke of gobbling up most of the bacon and the prawn sandwiches from the luxurious buffet table, much to everyone's amusement.

He was so handsome it was unfair. When he turned that killer smile on a woman it was as though he could see her secrets and make her feel like the most stunning person in the room.

But he had not even noticed that she was there.

Kyle was so totally natural in these surroundings, while she…she could just about hear the person next to her against the furious hum of chatter—if she leant close enough…

Suddenly she needed air, and a chance to think away from the barrage of broken sounds.

By squeezing past the elegantly dressed media executives by the door, who looked at her as if she was a creature from another much less stylish planet, where couture did not exist, Lulu made her way onto the sheltered decking outside the bar. The view was amazing. She leant on the edge of a metalwork table and looked out across the cold width of the Thames to hotels and the financial heart of the City of London. So many people—and they all seemed to know where they were going and what they wanted in life.

What was she doing here?

Mike was way too good at sweeping her along with his ideas. Of course she could do the basic admin on a non-fiction book. That was not a problem. She sorted out other people's financial records to pay her bills. But her mother's diaries and letters? That was a different matter.

How could she read those letters her mother had sent from Uganda in the last few months before she was killed? There had been a time when she'd used to run home from school to see if there was an envelope covered in brightly coloured stamps in the post. Not at the end. In those cold, bleak winter days she'd simply left them unopened in her father's studio, where he could have the private joy of reading them first.

She would find them later on the kitchen table. Treasured words to be savoured in a safe and warm place, far away from fighting and danger and disease.

Everything had changed on that last mission. Ruth had changed. Her mother had made a choice. And left her for the final time.

Going back to revisit that pain was not just a step into her past—it was bigger than one of the mountains Kyle Munroe was used to.

She was not ready to climb that mountain. She hadn't even reached base camp.

A gust of cold wind eddied around the wall and she shivered inside her suit. The weather had changed. Grey skies. Grey river.

She had her own life now. And more than enough work to do back home in Kingsmede. It was madness to even think of accepting Mike's offer. That connection to her past life had died with her father, and she had to move forward.

Time to go in and tell Mike that the answer was no. Kyle would have to write his book as best he could without her help. Perhaps there was another way? Was it possible for Kyle to use the diaries without her involvement and pay the hospice a fee? That might work.

Encouraged by having an alternative suggestion, she had just slipped in through the side entrance to the bar when she heard a loud, 'Marta?'

Lulu whirled around in surprise at the man's voice, and stepped back so quickly that the heel of one of her mules got stuck in a gap between the wide strips of wooden decking. As she tried to slip it back onto her foot the mule flipped up and landed on a table, happily unoccupied, clattering against the crockery. Lulu hopped over to the table to rescue her shoe before it could be held to ransom—only to find that Kyle Munroe had saved the day and got there before her.

Responding to the yelps from the waiters, Kyle gave a sudden whoop and snatched up the shoe before it could do any more damage. He shook his head when he saw who the shoe belonged to. 'I thought I recognised this rampaging item of footwear. This is starting to become a habit, Marta. Are you a secret stalker? I am honoured, of course, but should I be worried?'

'Sorry to disappoint you, but I'm here with Mike Baxter.'

He gave her a slight bow from the waist. 'How intriguing. In that case, I believe this is your glass slipper, madam. May I have the honour?'

Before Lulu knew what was happening, Kyle had dropped to his knees and her shoe was on the decking. A rough skinned hand gently wrapped around her left ankle and as though by magic Lulu found herself holding her leg in position so that Kyle could slide her backless shoe onto her foot.

As she tried to pull away, his fingers brushed the back of her calf through her thin black stockings, sending the most delicious shivers up her leg. Lulu instantly tried to move backwards to pull away from his grasp.

With the predictable result.

She overbalanced and found herself having to jerk forward to support her weight by pressing one hand onto each of Kyle's shoulders.

'Whoa! Steady there.'

Kyle was still on his knees as he looked up into her face. Their eyes locked.

And Lulu's world turned over. It was as though time had stopped and they were the only people on the riverbank. No sound except her own rapid breathing and Kyle's heartbeat. A beat she could sense through the gentle rise and fall of the muscular shoulders under her fingers.

Something at the bottom of her stomach clenched so hard she inhaled deeply.

He opened his mouth to say something, and then closed it again before giving her a half-smile with his eyes and mouth. A knowing smile.

Idiot, Lulu thought. *He knows exactly what he is doing and I fell for it.* So why did her stomach flip again when she looked at him?

It hit her with a very heavy thud that working close to this man every day could be *seriously* bad news. Yet another factor against the whole idea.

'Thank you. Again,' she managed to get out as Kyle stretched to his full height.

To her horror, Lulu realised that the whole sordid and humiliating scene had been acted out in full view of all the journalists and media company people, who were clearly sniggering behind their glasses of fizzy bottled water. And Mike Baxter. Whose lower lip was quivering so fast he had to be biting the inside of his cheek as he guided her inside, to a quiet table at the far end of the room.

Lulu narrowed her eyes, daring him to comment, but instead he pulled out her chair and waited until she was comfortable before going on.

'I'm sorry to have left you like that, Lulu, but the editors are pressing me for an answer about Ruth's diaries. This seems like as good time as any to get two of my favourite people together.'

'Then perhaps you ought to rescue your star?'

Lulu looked towards the bar, where Kyle was surrounded by a gaggle of tall leggy girls dressed in black and clearly revelling in the moment. As she turned away a beam of sunlight broke through the floor-to-ceiling glass windows, bringing his cheekbones and dark eye sockets into sharp focus. A little too sharply into focus.

'Has Kyle been ill, Mike?'

Mike nodded. 'Mmm. Not much misses you, does it?' He leant closer. 'The boy has lost weight. Chest infections are an occupational hazard, but this one is proving hard to treat. Oh, don't worry. He's responded well to the antibiotics, but it's going to take a while. Providing, of course…' he paused for a second and looked up as Kyle saun-tered in with two large steaming beakers of what smelt like tea '…I can hold him down long enough to take some rest.'

'Rest? Are you talking about me?' Kyle re-sponded with a chuckle, before placing one of the teas in front of Lulu. 'You should know better than that by now, Mike.' He glanced across at

Lulu before sitting next to Mike. 'Thought you looked a bit chilly out there, Marta. This should warm you up.'

'That's very thoughtful, Kyle.'

Mike looked from Kyle back to Lulu in surprise. 'I didn't know that you two had met before? How did that happen?'

'Oh, Marta and I are old friends. I think I should warn you to watch your back, Mike. This lady is on a secret mission of her own! I hope you don't have any precious artwork lying around the place.'

Mike shook his head. 'Whatever you have been drinking, stop now. And why are you calling her Marta? Do you have the faintest idea what this idiot is talking about, Lulu?'

'Lulu?' Kyle burst out laughing. 'Now, please—I expected a more convincing alias cover name than that!'

While Mike stared, open-mouthed, the lady in question decided to take control and casually tried her tea. 'Oh, it's all quite simple, really. Kyle and I have not been properly introduced.'

She lifted the beaker towards Kyle before taking

another sip. 'Congratulations on the book launch, Dr Munroe—it seems to have been a terrific success. And also thanks for the dedication. You see, my real name is Lulu Hamilton, and Ruth Taylor Hamilton was my mother. Apparently Lulu is an African word for *pearl*. Don't you think that's pretty?'

Kyle stared in mute horror at the extremely pretty blonde woman sitting across from him and was shocked into silence.

Never in his wildest dreams—and some of them could be pretty wild, even by his standards—had he imagined for one second that the inspirational surgeon he had worked with in Uganda could have another life as a wife and a mother.

Ruth Taylor Hamilton had been capable of it. He had no doubt about that. Except that she had never once ever mentioned she had a family back home. Not one word.

Other medics had had letters and photographs clipped to the walls of their tent, and he had envied them that many times, but not Ruth.

He glanced sideways at Mike Baxter, who simply nodded, and then dared to speak.

'I had no idea.'

'Ruth left her husband and daughter back in England, and that was the way she liked it. Two separate parts of her life. She never talked about Tom or Lulu when she was on a mission. That was her way of coping.'

Kyle took a couple of breaths before looking into the face of the girl who was apparently the daughter of the most amazing woman he had ever met.

He scanned her features. The lovely full bow of her upper lip, the high cheekbones sprinkled with freckles and the stunning blue eyes below fair eyebrows. And that hair!

But he couldn't see one single thing in her face that reminded him of Ruth.

'Kyle, mate. You're staring.'

Mike's voice startled him. He was right. He had been staring—and she knew it. His embarrassment was saved only by Lulu herself.

'It's okay, Kyle. I'm used to being compared to the famous Ruth Taylor Hamilton. It goes with the territory. I gave up on being upset about the disappointment in other people's eyes a long time ago. I know that I have my dad's colouring—and I'm definitely not the heroic type. In fact, didn't you think I was a librarian?'

Mike groaned and dropped his head into his hands.

'I'm very sorry for your loss, Miss Hamilton. Your mother was a remarkable woman. I apologise if I offended you, and… Is that your phone?'

Lulu dived into her messenger bag, where her cellphone was flashing away, and quickly checked the caller ID. *Drat.*

'Sorry, Mike, I have to take this. Why don't you tell Kyle about your crazy idea? I shouldn't be long.' She went outside again.

She'd lied. The text message was from an estate agent in the town closest to her home village of Kingsmede.

A month ago, after a hard look at her finances, she had taken the tough decision to tell the local agencies that she might be interested in renting out the huge family house she had lived in all of her life.

Big mistake. Since then she had been inundated with calls on a weekly basis. Now, apparently, a family with four small children were interested in renting the house for the next twelve months. Only there was a catch. They needed to move in six weeks. They were willing to pay the full rental rate and a cash deposit. Could she be out by then?

Her fingers hesitated on the keypad. She desperately needed that rental income if she had any chance of going to art college, but six weeks was not long to finish clearing the huge house. And it would mean leaving her home just before Christmas.

Lulu pressed her thumb and third finger hard against her eyebrows.

She wasn't ready. This was what she had planned—only she had not expected it to happen so quickly.

Before she changed her mind, she quickly created a message expressing her apologies and pressed the 'send' button. A few seconds later she received a text of thanks from the agent.

Next year. That was it. She would make a start in January. In the meantime she would have to sell more paintings and work longer hours as a bookkeeper. She could do it.

Someone came up alongside her and leant on the metal railing a few feet away.

It was Kyle.

She half turned, and was about to explain that she could not possibly work on his project when he started talking in the same voice he had used at the table when he'd discovered who she was. Serious. Sincere. Intense. Adorable. A voice she could not interrupt.

'Two months ago I lost a very special patient. A little girl. Lakshmi was the daughter of my friends who run the field clinic. Most of the community are Buddhists. They refuse to kill any living creature, including the packs of wild dogs that roam the villages looking for food. Lakshmi was a typical five-year-old—bright, always laughing, and she loved puppies.'

Kyle looked out across the river as he talked.

'We don't know when she was bitten by a rabid

dog, but by the time the first symptoms appeared it was too late to save her. If she had been vaccinated she might have stood a small chance of lasting out long enough to survive the treatment. She hadn't.'

He turned sideways and looked at her directly. 'I have the job of choosing who gets the vaccines and who doesn't. There simply isn't enough for everyone.' He glanced back to the bar and all of the busy, healthy people going about their lives. 'That's why I'm here today. That's why I agreed to write this book. It's not about me; it's about the patients and what they need. Every penny goes to the foundation.'

Lulu lifted her head before replying. 'And this second book will pay for the vaccines you need?'

He nodded. 'The first book paid to build and equip a complete clinic, and the paperback should pay the wages for the next few years. I have Mike and the TV company to thank for that. I'm just a jobbing medic. I like to keep things simple.'

She was not ready for the feel of his cold, long

rough-skinned working fingers that meshed with hers as she clasped hold of the railing.

'Mike thinks that you are the best person to help me. My patients need those drugs. If I have to get down on my knees and beg you to help, I will. Because I cannot go back to that clinic and tell them that other children could suffer like that little girl.'

He moved closer to her, face to face, and his fingers locked onto hers, leaving his thumb to move seductively across her wrist.

'I have the feeling that you might like to see a man beg. Am I right?'

She locked onto those hazel-green eyes with their tiny creases and her heart melted. She smiled when she didn't want to.

'That rather depends on what he's begging for.'

'Quite a lot, actually. Apparently I have three weeks to produce this book if I want to have it ready for March publication. I need all the help I can get! Ruth's diaries would make a huge difference. Ten years is a long time ago. And did I mention that I am a two-finger typist?'

That knocked the wind out of her sails for a few

moments, and he could almost see the cogs in her brain working overtime before she nodded. 'Before I agree to anything, I do have a couple of conditions.'

He tilted his head slightly to one side, his heavy brows coming together in concentration. 'Fire away.'

'First, I would prefer that the diaries did not leave my home. So if you want to read them, then you'll have to come to see *me* in Kingsmede. Not the other way around.'

'Done. Next?' His eyes had not broken focus.

She faltered slightly and fought to regain control of her voice. 'I work best on my own, so it would make sense if Mike could send me everything you have from that time, plus any official records. If you can give me a week to sort it all out the best I can, then you can decide whether there is enough material to write the book. Or not. How does that sound?'

Kyle pursed his lips tight together before replying. 'A week? That might work. I'll need to dig out what I have from Africa, and I have this

book tour to take care of. There is also some…
well, personal stuff— But, yes.' He nodded. 'A
week could work out very well.'

Her eyes locked onto his eyes, and she kept
them there until he sighed and nodded.

'Okay. It makes sense to sort through the bulk
of the work in one session. I'll soon find out what
I am missing.' His head lifted. 'I'll do my best.'

Lulu stared him down. 'Does that mean you'll
do it? You'll come to Kingsmede and work with
me—starting next Sunday for two weeks?'

'Absolutely. You help me with my book, and I'll
make it the tribute that Ruth Taylor Hamilton
deserves. I'll be happy to shout about it from the
rooftops when the time is right. So, Miss
Hamilton…' He paused and squeezed her right
hand a little tighter. 'Do we have a deal?'

Lulu inhaled deeply, took in the unshaven upper
lip and the solid square stubbly jawline of the
smiling face in front of her, and closed her eyes
for a second before nodding.

'I'm not sure if I can do this, and it is one huge
risk, but, yes, Dr Munroe, we have a deal.'

He brought her fingers to his lips for a fleeting second before releasing her.

'In that case—' he shuffled his jacket closed '—it's time to get down to the really important business of the day.'

Lulu held her breath, hardly daring to imagine what he had in mind.

'I have been dreaming about a huge British fry-up for the last six months. Care to join me?'

# CHAPTER FOUR

LULU popped her pins and threads back inside her sewing kit and smoothed down the seam of the printed floor-length curtain so that the repair was invisible from inside the room.

Even in the faint autumn sunlight Lulu knew every pleat of the fabric where the sunshine had faded the pattern of bright yellow overblown roses to a dark cream. Her parents had never been able to afford to replace the curtains her grandmother had bought years earlier. Not with so many windows. Not in a house this size. Even her godmother Emma Carmichael had mentioned that surely it was time to change them before the winter.

A cool draft swirled the curtains, and Lulu suppressed a shiver that ran across her shoulders and down her back.

The unused dining room had been the obvious place to spread out the boxes of documents that Mike Baxter had sent over, but it was a cold, north-facing room and she had not lit the open fire in years. Time to change that.

Kyle might be used to the snows of Nepal, but she wasn't.

Lulu plumped up the cushions on the chesterfield sofa next to the fireplace, then turned to face the long, narrow antique dining table that ran the length of the room. The polished surface was hidden below neat parallel rows of folders.

One individual folder for each of the nine months that Kyle Munroe had spent in Uganda ten years earlier.

Mike had apologised in advance for the fact that the storage crates of records and files were 'a tad unorganised', but she had been unprepared for just how much of a mess they truly were.

It was only when the boxes of jumbled papers had arrived on the Tuesday morning following the book launch that the enormity of the task she was facing had begun to truly hit home.

It had taken her every spare minute for the last week, but she had done the best she could.

In a world and culture where computers had been a distant dream, the original records from Uganda were a jumble of single pages of hand-written notes, record cards with patient informa-tion, copies of invoices... In fact anything and everything that the foundation had saved from the Uganda mission for the last year or so before Kyle had been flown home.

Somehow all these simple pieces of paper seemed more intimate than an anonymous computer record or database. The hand that had created these marks on paper belonged to a living human being, and each piece seemed to have picked up some of the personality of the person who had created it.

Almost like the style of an artist, there was no mistaking who had written, or in many cases scribbled, the information. She had scanned through hundreds of separate pages over the last

few days to check for dates, and some person-
alities shone through.

Kyle Munroe, for example.

Lulu picked up an undated but signed medical
report from a crate of bits and pieces labelled
*'Undated'* that only Kyle would be able to place.
The handwriting was strong, direct and fervent,
in long straight strokes and clear, concise
language. Always in black ink. The man might
have looked more than a little scruffy at the tube
station, but the Kyle who had created these
records was focused and organised. Professional.

Mike had already told her that Kyle would be
bringing his personal diary with him in person,
and yet there was so much of his personality in
the box she was looking at now she felt that the
diary would be almost too much.

She slipped the report back into the crate and
her foot connected with a dilapidated old
holdall with the letters KBM stencilled onto the
cover.

It did not look too different from the rucksack
she had seen Kyle carrying on the underground

in London. And yet she had held back from opening up this bag.

It felt too private and too personal for anyone but Kyle to open.

Of course Emma had laughed at her, and accused her of simply being scared of what she might find inside. Frightened of the unknown. Right, as always.

Kyle Munroe remained an unknown entity.

She certainly did not recall hearing the name Kyle Munroe until Mike had told her about him. Perhaps her father had known about the new medics who had been recruited in that last year when she'd been away at university? It certainly wasn't something he would have talked to her about. Those last few months were a complete mystery. Just as much as Kyle himself.

Perhaps that was why she had taken the time to read *Medicine Man* and find out more about the work in Nepal. She had even visited his website.

The man in the book looked like the same man that she had met in London. There was no mistaking that.

Except that Kyle probably did not recognise how much of his personality came through the short posts he created every week on his blog. The humour. The dedication. The charm. She could well understand why the book and the TV documentary had become so popular. He was beguiling, and yet completely true to himself.

The thought of an emergency medic like Kyle sitting next to her at this table sent unfamiliar tremors of excitement direct to her cheeks, and instantly she felt the blood rush to skin. She had felt the fluttering sensation bubble up over the past few days, until the thought of actually seeing him again face to face was starting to make her nervous.

Skittery.

And she did not do skittery.

Not normally. Not ever. There was just something about this man. She actually *wanted* to see him again. Or was it the man in the book she wanted to meet? There was only one way to find out.

And he was due to arrive in—oh, a couple of hours.

A sudden flash of colour on the other side of

the glass broke her thoughts, and Lulu looked up to see a young red setter running around the lawn to the trees.

Belle—the red setter puppy that her godmother Emma had given her for a Christmas present. Belle was totally adorable, and her constant companion, but a boisterous dog and official paperwork were not a good combination, and Lulu was happy for her pet to exhaust herself in the huge garden instead of indoors.

Lulu smiled to herself and shook her head as she watched the madcap antics of the silly animal as Belle scampered and jumped around.

She was being an idiot. Mike Baxter had asked her to sort the files and paperwork into date order and she had done the best she could. Kyle should have no problem connecting his own diary pages with the records to create the background history for his book. And the sooner that was done, the sooner he would be out of Kingsmede and she could get back to her ordinary life.

This was simply a few days of work for both of

them. Nothing more. And then the hospice would have the new respite unit they needed.

Tomorrow she would start reading through her mother's diaries. Tomorrow or the next day.

As for the personal letters? Well, that was a different matter.

Lulu turned her head away from the window and caught sight of her reflection in the silvered Venetian mirror above the fireplace. She stroked back her hair behind her left ear, so that her hearing aid was in full view.

She didn't need archived records to remind herself of what had happened in Africa. She saw the direct evidence every morning when she looked in the bathroom mirror, and every evening when she removed her hearing aid and reconciled herself to the fact that she would never hear again the things she'd once loved.

She lived with the memory every single day of her life.

The doctors had told her many times that she was very lucky to have survived the mysterious tropical infection that had robbed her of her hearing in that one ear. She still had her brain, and enough hearing in the other ear to enjoy life to the full.

Her father had brought her home and sat with her for days, only leaving her side when Emma had come over. It was probably the longest period of time that they had ever spent in the same room together.

Except of course he'd known that he was not the parent she wanted to see. Lulu remembered how she'd kept asking the same question of her father, the doctors—in fact, anyone who came into her room. Where was her mother? Why wasn't her mother there? She had repeated the question over and over again. Which only showed how ill she must have been. Because her mother had been in Uganda, and that had meant she might as well have been on another planet. Out of reach.

Lulu slowly uncurled her hair back over her ear.

No. She didn't need a diary to remind her of where her mother had worked and what she had been doing all those years ago. It was staring her in the face every day.

A series of playful barks on the other side of the patio door made her smile.

Poor Belle had been neglected. Time to make amends.

This was her life now. And it was up to her to make the best of it.

Kyle Munroe swung the Range Rover slowly around the bend from the narrow lane, his eyes scanning from side to side until he spotted a small hand-painted sign attached to a stone pillar. Taylor House. This was it. He had come to the right place.

Thanks to the satellite navigation system on Mike's car, and a very helpful lady walking a dog, he had found it.

The four-wheel-drive car slowed, and he pulled up on the wide gravel drive which circled around the front entrance of an imposing Georgian stone house, complete with narrow, square windows and a fine collection of chimneys. A decorative stone porch was lit up with bright pots of pink cyclamens and a pair of bay trees, either side of a very solid-looking wooden door painted in an elegant shade of dark navy.

His smart boots crunched into the gravel as he swung down from the leather seat and slowly uncurled his body into something like a standing position.

The drive from his father's flat in London had taken a lot longer than he had expected, and his body was paying the price. He raised his right arm above his head to release the tension in his neck.

Fractured vertebrae and strained ligaments and tendons did not heal overnight. Or at least they didn't in his case.

Maybe Mike was right. Perhaps he should cut back on his treks to remote clinics this year and focus on getting back into shape? His arm was only the latest of many little accidents he had laughed off over the years.

It was so frustrating. He wanted to be doing *more* aerobic exercise, building his lung capacity. Not less. He could not let this infection beat him. Not this time—not ever. He would carry on taking the antibiotics. He would clear his lungs. Persistent chest infections were a risk in his work. An occupational hazard. But it had certainly put a damper on his plans to extend the vaccine programme.

Kyle pushed his spine out, and looked up through the wide-open branches of the copper beech and oak trees above his head. Blackbirds and robins hopped from dripping branch to dripping branch.

So what if he did miss the English seasons? He sniffed and wrapped his father's scarf tighter around his neck. The people here had never seen the wild rhododendron forests in the Himalayas. Smelt the soil after the summer monsoon.

A grey squirrel scampered across the wet grass at the side of the house to scrabble among the fallen leaves. Kyle smiled. He had forgotten how much he missed such familiar things.

He looked up at the house, with its imposing neat front gardens. Open farmland spread out in all directions, broken by copses of woodland and a distant line of trees where black rooks were calling out to one another.

It was hard to believe that Ruth Taylor

Hamilton had grown up and lived here, on the edge of a small country village in the South of England. Suddenly he was struck with a vivid memory of the last time he'd seen Ruth. Jumping into an ambulance just like on any other hot African morning. A quick wave to the local children and she'd been gone, in a cloud of red dust on the dirt road, before he'd even had a chance to speak to her.

And in that moment his life had changed. Yes, they had been working close to a war zone, but nobody could have predicted that only two hours later her ambulance would drive over a land mine on the way to the village clinic.

He shivered, and sniffed once more before crunching his way to the porch.

That had been ten years ago, and a world away from where he was standing now.

He had come to do a job, and part of that job was honouring Ruth—and that was what he intended to do. Her daughter need never know the terrible secret about what had truly happened that morning.

That thought made him stop and pull his hand

away from the doorbell. Why had Ruth never told anyone that she had a daughter and a husband back in England? Living in this very house? He could have done something when he'd got back to London. Visited? Tried to appease his guilt in some way?

Of course he had never thought to ask Mike Baxter about Ruth's family, and he had not kept in contact with the other medical workers when they'd been disbanded to various missions around the world.

Well, it was not too late. And now Lulu was on her own he owed it to Ruth to make sure that her only daughter had everything she needed. It was the least he could do, seeing as he owed Ruth Taylor Hamilton his life.

Just as Kyle stretched out to press the brass doorbell there was a commotion in the direction of the squirrel he had just been looking at, and he turned just in time to see a red setter hurtling through the grass. The playful dog pounced, and pounced again, but her target was already halfway up the oak tree.

Kyle chuckled to himself as he strolled around the side of the house and called out to the dog.

'Hello, there! Not much luck with that one.'

The dog froze for all of two seconds, before bounding towards him and launching herself onto his trousers, yapping and trying to lick him so furiously that Kyle could not resist any longer. He swept the dog up into his arms. Her gangly red limbs and sharp nails scrabbled for purchase, but the muddy dog's muzzle, fur and paws had already done enough damage.

A sharp whistle echoed around the drive, and the red setter turned into a frantic bag of bones and fur that Kyle struggled to lower to the ground. This bundle of fun was in too much of a hurry, and soon squirmed her way out of his arm-lock to race away around the corner of the house.

With a shake of his head, Kyle shrugged up the collar of his coat and followed her. Perhaps the lady of the house was outside? The gravel crunched under his feet as he turned the corner, hands in his pockets. Then he stopped. Frozen into position by the scene being acted out in front of him.

On the other side of the flowerbeds and neat lawn, the woman he now knew was Lulu Hamilton was leaping from one foot to the other as she held a piece of twig high in the air, playing and pretending to fight off the loving and energetic attentions of the floppy red setter, who was jumping just as high and clearly having just as much fun as the blonde.

Suddenly content to simply watch in silence, Kyle leant on the corner of the house as Lulu threw the stick far across to the tall trees and turned back to an open bonfire.

With a single smooth and practised motion, Lulu lifted a small handsaw and cut through a branch of dry wood. Then again. Small twigs were thrown into a metal fire basket which glowed red and orange as the flames licked upwards, hotter and higher.

But it was Lulu herself who held him spellbound.

Her arms moved smoothly back and forth, collecting large logs into a crate. The glow from the burning embers shone back from her face in the fading light, and her blond corkscrew curls were scrunched back into a rough ponytail held away from her forehead with a striped bandana.

Her fine high cheekbones glowed pink with spontaneous energy and a sense of natural warmth and fun as she vigorously rubbed the dog's head before throwing another twig. The dull grey suit was gone. Replaced with faded jeans and a padded jacket over what looked like a man's check shirt.

She looked confident, self-sufficient, and totally in control in this space.

The Lulu Hamilton he had met in London had been pretty and intelligent, but also guarded and ill at ease with the grandiose plans that Mike had come up with.

This version of Lulu Hamilton was mesmerising.

She had such a sense of smiling joy in her simple task. She looked like a woman who was accustomed to chopping her own wood, content with the company of a mad dog and a burning fire.

One thing was certain. He had been expecting to meet a pretty blonde in a suit. What he saw instead was a stunningly beautiful woman with a style and body that no man could ignore. Which probably meant trouble.

This was Ruth's daughter, and he had a responsibility—perhaps even an obligation—to make sure that she was cared for.

He could have looked at her all day and not regretted it for one moment. Except the dog had other ideas, spotted him, and decided that it was time for Kyle to join in their game.

Lulu threw the last of the parchment-dry ancient newspapers her father had hoarded onto the fire, brushed down her gloves, and stood back to watch the white-hot flames flare up into the damp air.

This part of her garden looked out over the farmland leading down to Kingsmede, and she could just see the lights from the thatched cottages that were scattered around the old church with its familiar steeple. It was a dreamy scene of soft lights and faint misty air.

She loved this view. This was the only home she had ever known and the only one she ever wanted. Even if it meant renting the house out for a while when she was at art college, it would be here for her to return to.

That truly did make her smile and, picking up one final branch, she turned to see what new garden creature Belle had found to torment.

And stepped back in startled shock and surprise.

The most handsome man she had ever seen in her life was leaning against the wall of her house, only a few feet away from where she was standing. Watching her in silence.

Was she dreaming?

It was Kyle Munroe. The same man whose paperwork she has just been reading. Only this version of Kyle bore no relationship whatsoever to the skinny young medical student in a pop group T-shirt in the colour photos from his book. Her stomach decided to behave like a tumble drier. Skittery did not even come close.

She might have thought that Kyle was attractive that Friday afternoon in London, but this man was from another planet.

The dirty long hair had been expertly cut. Clean shiny brown layers lay flat around his ears, swept

away from his cleanshaven face so that the prominent square jawline and the long, straight nose
were the first things she saw.

Without his beard the square jaw was so angled
it might have been sculpted. But it was his mouth
that knocked the air out of her lungs and had her
clinging onto the log pile for support. It was a
mouth made for smiling, with slight dimples
either side.

The corners of those amazing eyes crinkled
slightly, and Lulu realised that he had been
watching her as his smile widened. Despite the
real fire close at hand, the warmth of that smile
seemed to heat the air between them. It was so
full of genuine charm and delight that she knew,
no matter what, that this was the smile that would
stay with her whenever she thought of Kyle.

Only now, at this moment, the smile was for
*her*. Her heart leapt. More than a little. And just
enough for her to recognise that the blush of heat
racing through her neck and face were not only
due to the flames warming her back.

At this distance in the fading light, his eyes

were dark, scrunched up by the deep crease of his smile as he strolled across the grass towards her, Belle scampering around his legs. She knew that those eyes were mostly hazel brown, with flakes of forest-green, but for now all she could see were a pair of heavy dark eyebrows.

If she had ever imagined that Kyle Munroe could not possibly be more attractive than the photo on the cover of his book, then she had been wrong. The top two buttons of his pale blue shirt stretched open as the fabric strained to cover a broad chest, revealing a hit of deeply tanned skin and more than a few dark chest hairs.

He was stunning.

*Oh, no. Do not stare at his chest. Just don't.*

The pounding of her heart was simply because she had been taken by surprise—that was all. Trying desperately to regain some kind of control over feelings that were new and raw, Lulu was suddenly aware that she was standing there with a tree branch still in her hand, and casually she moved forward to throw it onto the fire before returning his smile and turning to meet him.

Luckily he spoke first, his voice low and husky in the quiet garden as he smiled and reached out his hand. Lulu shucked off her glove and felt long, cold fingers clasp hers for only a few seconds before she released him. The callused surfaces of his fingers rasped against the skin on the back of her hand. Gentle, but firm. And surprisingly very different from the handshake they had shared in the London taxi cab only a week earlier. Now his fingers seemed to linger and slide over hers, as though they wanted to maintain contact for as long as possible.

No complaints from her end on that point.

'Miss Hamilton. Sorry if I startled you. I tried the front door, but your burglar alarm found me first.' He nodded towards Belle, who was snuffling around their feet. 'Apologies for being so late. Not used to the traffic. But it's great to be here at last. Do you mind if I make use of your fire?'

In the fraction of a second it took Kyle to stroll over to the fire and stretch out his hands towards the flames, inappropriate and totally crazy thoughts about the effect those same fingers could have on other parts of her body flitted through Lulu's mind.

No need for flames on this side of the fire. *Oh, dear.*

Lulu inhaled deeply, straightened her back, and managed to find her voice at last as she smiled back at him. 'Please do. It *is* feeling chilly. Mike warned me that your timing was flexible, so no problem. And please call me Lulu.'

Belle sidled up to Kyle and tried to push her nose into the side pocket of his trousers.

Lulu laughed out loud. 'You'll have to excuse Belle. She is totally spoiled and has already worked out that pockets are designed to hold treats.' To prove the point, she reached into her own jacket pocket and pulled out a dog biscuit, which Belle pounced on. 'Let's get inside before she notices we're gone. How does hot coffee sound?'

'It sounds wonderful. I've left something in the car. Back in a moment.'

Kyle jogged back to the Range Rover, scooped up the bakery bag and got back just in time to follow Lulu onto a wide stone patio with garden furniture which led to a dark green door at the back of the house.

Lulu turned the handle and swung the door wide as she shucked off her boots in the long porch. 'Please go through. Welcome to Taylor House.'

# CHAPTER FIVE

KYLE walked past Lulu into what would have passed for an art gallery rather than a kitchen.

The riot of bright colours was so totally unexpected he almost recoiled at the sensory overload. The contrast between the cold grey garden and the exotic chaos of colour was shocking, and he turned back to his hostess with an expression of awe.

'Wow! This is like no other kitchen I've ever been in. Are you the artist?'

Lulu smiled across at him as she unbuttoned her jacket. 'Not guilty. My father spent a lot of time working on abstracts. He loved colour and hated change.' She shrugged her shoulders before filling the kettle, determined to settle her jangled nerves with the familiar world of her kitchen. 'I could have painted over it, I suppose, but it is distinctive.'

Lulu watched Kyle step slowly around the kitchen, grinning and peering closer at the images on the walls, before picking up a purple pottery pig dotted with bright splodges of yellow and red. Long, delicate surgeon's fingers moved over the model, lovingly caressing the little pig, and Lulu gulped down something very close to jealousy.

When he finally looked up at her his face was alive with delight, and an energy so totally unexpected that she almost dropped the cups she was holding when he spoke.

'Please don't paint over it. It reminds me of Nepal. Brilliant! I love it.' He stepped away to loll against the wall, so that he faced Lulu as she busied herself with cups and coffee. 'I can see now how you came to the art world. No orchids, though. Do you have a special room for those? I had been wondering if you forge them yourself or have someone else do it for you?'

'Orchids?' Thank heavens for a change in the subject. 'Oh, of course—the gallery! Yes, I confess, I forge them myself. I'm surprised you remembered that.'

'Yellow orchids. How could I forget? Please— let me help you with that.'

Kyle took the tray from Lulu's hands before she could protest, and carried it over to the old pine kitchen table where she had been sorting through family photographs.

'Are you sure you can manage? I see the plaster cast is missing. How is your wrist?'

A rapid shake and flex of his strapped-up arm was his answer. 'It still needs work. Luckily Mike has an automatic car I can borrow for the week, so I am mobile—but thank you for the thought.'

He flashed her a half-smile, his wide mouth creaking into a lady-killer grin, practised over the years to ensure any female within his target radius would melt into radioactive decay in seconds.

Something strange happened to Lulu's stomach and her legs felt a little wobbly. No lunch. That was it. And the warmth spreading from her neck to her face was just the natural result of being taken by surprise. She tried to hide it by gathering together the photographs as Kyle continued.

'Speaking of Mike—I come bearing gifts from a certain patisserie which apparently you are fond of.'

'Gifts?' she asked, trying not to sound too keen, despite the bag of hares that had started kickboxing inside her stomach.

'Chocolate cake. As some form of compensation for the terrible mess my paperwork must be in.'

He held the bag out towards her, and a scrumptious smell wafted into the kitchen.

'I can assure you that your paperwork cannot be any worse than Mike's—but he does know my weaknesses.'

Lulu pursed her lips and gracefully accepted the bag from Kyle's fingers before bowing slightly in his direction. She could take a bribe now and again. And it gave her something to do with her hands, which were starting to crease the photographs with their pressure.

'That was very thoughtful. Won't you sit?'

She stepped back and flicked on lights as Kyle followed her to the table.

'Thank you,' he replied with a shrug, 'but my old bones need to stretch. Not used to sitting in one place for very long. This really is a lovely room. Oh, I'm sorry. I'm obviously disturbing your paperwork.'

Still spread out across the pine table was the rest of the jumble of old photographs, mostly black and white, and several storage boxes.

Lulu glanced back towards him from under her eyelashes as she unwrapped the deep, dense dark chocolate ganache cake. 'I was looking for a few family photographs you could use in the book. I always intended to put them into albums, but somehow never got around to it.'

'Well, I know that feeling. My dad has crates of my stuff stashed in his apartment. It took me the best part of an hour to find what I had saved from Uganda.'

Aware that Kyle was leaning one handed against the dresser, she gestured towards the kitchen table.

'Some cake, perhaps, to go with your coffee?'

'Thanks, but the cake is for you. I'm not used to rich food.'

She watched as he perched on the edge of the table, only a few feet away from her, so that his long legs inside smart jeans could stretch out in front of him. He looked so at home. Casual. Relaxed. And clearly oblivious to the fact that his taut thigh muscles were straining against the fabric of the trousers.

Lulu felt herself blushing, the heat starting around her neck as she turned away to pour the coffee. It was certainly time to deflect this conversation. By moving back to her chair at the table, she was able to cradle her mug of coffee and divert his attention.

'How do you feel about being back here in Britain, Kyle? Away from the clinic in Nepal?'

He turned so that he could see her side view.

'You must miss them enormously.' Lulu replied. 'Your patients, I mean.' And kicked herself for being so tongue-tied.

How did he do it?

She was not normally so clumsy. She had never, ever felt so awkward and tongue tied and adolescent around a man in her life. And this was *her* kitchen! How was she going to survive two weeks of having Kyle Munroe in her life?

If Kyle had noticed her awkwardness he did not show it as he smiled across at her, raised his coffee with one hand and waved his injured wrist in the air a couple of times. 'Ten weeks ago I was making my way through ice and snow down to the treeline when our ambulance was caught in a rockfall. We all slid out more or less in one piece. Now I'm sitting in this delightful kitchen in warmth and comfort. I consider myself very fortunate to be here. My patients are in excellent hands—but, yes, I do miss the people. Very much.'

Kyle reached forward and picked up one of the photographs from the table. A slim, handsome blond man in brightly coloured clothing was standing next to a large abstract painting, his arms wrapped around the shoulders of two other young men.

All three were laughing into the camera through bearded faces.

'Is this one of your relatives? He certainly has your colouring.'

Lulu casually accepted the photo from Kyle's hand, as though she had not seen it before. 'Oh, that's my father—Tom Hamilton. There were a couple of exhibitions of his work when he was at art school. Those lads with him in the crazy hippy gear are some of his mates from university. Apparently it was a wild time—and, no, I don't know what they got up to.'

There was a knowing chuckle from across the table.

'Mike told me that he had passed away. I'm very sorry. He must have been fun to live with. Was he a forger, as well?'

Lulu flashed a glance into Kyle's face, anxious to see if there was a hint of irony. Finding a genuine smile in place, she was totally disarmed by it. Of course there was no way that he could possibly know how hard living with Tom Hamilton had been.

'Not at all. Only the genuine article.' She smiled.

She was horrified to see her hand tremble just a little as Kyle focused the full heat of his attention on her. If only he was not dominating this small space! And so close to her. She had to regain control. Time to get down to business. The dining room. She could make sure that there was plenty of space between them in that room.

She lowered her beaker and scooped up the prints back into the box. 'Do you want to start work tonight?' she asked casually, trying to sound as though it was something she did every day. 'I've tried to collate everything Mike sent me from the official records into some sort of date order, but there are quite a few things where I have no clue. It's all laid out in the next room, any time you are ready.'

He leant his head slightly to one side. 'Absolutely. Although I do need to ask a favour of you before I see exactly what I have got myself into.'

'A favour?' Lulu frowned and half closed her eyes in pretend seriousness. She sat back in her chair. So he had an agenda after all. 'You are welcome to ask. After all, you did bring cake. Please go ahead.'

He turned his body so that he was directly across the table from her now, the full strength and force of his energy and personality focused on her small face. Burning into her skin. Demanding her total attention.

'I admired your mother very much. I meant what I said in my dedication. Stitch was an inspiration to me. Which is why I want this second book to be as much her story as it is mine. And I need your help to do that.'

Kyle gazed across at her and smiled as he stared into pale blue eyes the colour of a winter sky.

'When Mike introduced us last week I don't think I was very polite. For that I apologise. I could try and blame jet lag, but I always have been a bull in a china shop. I truly had no idea that Ruth had a daughter. So…' He clasped the back of the wooden chair, the knuckles of both hands white with the pressure. 'Here is my problem. I want to be back in Nepal in two weeks. Is there any way I could persuade you to spend more time with me so we can turn this book around in less than ten days? Please? Just tell me what I need to do to convince you, and I'm all yours.'

Lulu sat back in her kitchen chair and stared open mouthed at Kyle, who simply slid his delicious bottom onto the seat of the chair. She had certainly not intended to give this book one hundred percent of her time for the next two weeks. On the other hand, the sooner they finished the work, the sooner Kyle would be out of her life and she could get back to her normal quiet existence again. Which was what she wanted, wasn't it?

Drat this man for making her poor brain spin. Ten days? It might be possible, but there was a lot of material to work through.

'Do you know what you're asking?' she finally managed to blurt out.

Kyle waved one hand and shook his head. 'No clue. Like I said, I am a two-finger typist and proud. I can just about manage e-mails, and a few paragraphs a week, but everything else is handwritten. Pathetic, I know, but that is the truth. Which is why I need your help.'

And then he played his winning card. He turned on his best smouldering smile. Full beam. Maximum strength.

That was it. She couldn't hold it in any longer.

Lulu burst out laughing. 'Do you actually get results with that type of pathetic pleading about being a two-finger typist?'

'Well…yes. I don't find many girls who turn me down.' His face twisted in mock horror. 'Was it truly that bad? I haven't had complaints before.'

She nodded.

'You really thought that I was pathetic?'

She nodded.

Kyle collapsed back against the kitchen chair. 'Crashed and burned. Maybe I *have* been out of this country too long.'

He shrugged and smiled at her apologetically. Suddenly his bravado disappeared in a puff of smoke, along with his playful attitude. The shadows under his eyes and his prominent cheekbones seemed to be even more pronounced without the permanent smile. Or perhaps that was the low-energy lightbulbs that Lulu had fitted to save on the electricity bill?

The change in him was so sudden it was as though someone had turned a light off inside his body. He looked exhausted. And probably was.

She decided to take pity on him and bring that smile back. The room seemed a lot darker without it.

'Don't worry; you haven't lost your touch. Your male ego is still intact, but there are two very good reasons why your plea was doomed from the start.'

Leaning her arms on the table, Lulu leant forward and looked into that beautiful strong and masculine face. His hazel eyes were totally focused on her, and for a second she resisted the urge to look away from the intensity of that gaze. The long dark eyelashes fluttered slightly. She was only inches away from him, and in that small space there was so much unspoken feeling that she almost sensed he knew what she was going to say before the words formed.

'First, I enjoy sorting out other people's paperwork so much that people actually pay me to be their bookkeeper. I like it and I'm good at it. You don't, and apparently you aren't. Fact. You are going to find it hard to keep up with me.'

She let that sink in, and for a moment—just a

moment—saw something change in Kyle's face. Perhaps a glimpse of a suppressed smile? As though he was unaccustomed to having someone agree that he did not excel in all areas of his life?

Suddenly she needed an excuse so that she did not have to look at him, and she busied her hands with a completely unnecessary rearrangement of the beakers on the tray as she topped up his coffee. 'Secondly, I already know that you are only doing this book so that your patients can get the vaccines they need. Not for some personal ego trip or to fund your new yacht.' She flicked her eyes up to his. 'You don't have a yacht already, do you?'

Kyle bit his lower lip and shook his head emphatically in reply.

She paused, aware that she had his full attention. 'That's why I had already decided that *if* there is time—' she held up one hand for emphasis '—I *might* be able to help you with any typing you need to finish the book. It has nothing to do with you,' she added quickly. 'Just a sound business decision. The hospice needs those funds as soon as possible.'

He gazed into her face, slack-jawed, and smiled with a sincere warmth she had only glimpsed before. A real smile of genuine feeling that simply took her breath away.

He meant it. For that fraction of a second it was as though she had been given the key to look inside him and see the real Kyle beneath the façade. Outward bravado disguised a man capable of very deep feeling. And it surprised and intrigued her.

This was not the media star she had seen in London. This was more the man whose personality had shone through in his first book. She had misjudged him.

He truly was amazing.

Kyle raised both hands in submission, leant across the table, and with a grin as wide as the kitchen door said, 'Thank you.'

'You are most welcome. But don't thank me quite yet,' Lulu replied as she stood up and tugged down on the hem of her shirt to straighten it. 'You do still have to do the work. Even if it is one paragraph at a time. Using two fingers.' She looked across at him and gestured with her head towards the corridor. 'So, Dr Munroe, since you are in such a hurry to get back to the ice and snow, are you ready to get started?'

'After you. I'll bring my coffee and… Wow!'

Kyle stood at the door to the dining room, his beaker of coffee in one hand and his mouth open as he looked in shock and awe at the boxes and folders spread out across the long table.

'Perhaps we should start this tomorrow,' he whispered, and pretended to slink off back down the corridor on tiptoe to the kitchen.

Lulu shook her head and, throwing caution to the wind, hooked her hand around an elbow and drew him into the narrow room.

'It's okay. Don't panic just yet. Let me show you what I have been working on this last week.'

Lulu pointed towards the first set of folders as Kyle stood next to her, their arms still linked.

'Nine folders. One for each month that you were in Africa.'

Carefully sliding her arm out, with all of the

casual *this sort of thing happens every day* nonchalance she could muster, Lulu was free of him. She licked her dry lips and picked up the first dossier.

'Mike Baxter sent over crates of official records. Most of it was a jumble of single pages, but I tried to focus on anything and everything which links to a specific month. I hope that's okay?'

She watched as Kyle flipped open the file and started scanning down the top page before chuckling out loud. 'Okay? It's amazing. You know, I actually remember that.' He looked up into Lulu's face and hit her with that heart-stopping smile. 'We were expecting a delivery of dried mango. Only there was a mix up at the warehouse and we were all eating macaroni for three months. It was wonderful—that pasta probably saved more lives than I did.' With a shrug, and a self-deprecating wistful grin, he looked down the full length of the table before giving a low whistle. 'Did you really do all of this on your own?'

'It wasn't too bad. But I haven't opened your personal rucksack. You will want to do that on your own.'

He winced in reply. 'Do I get any special dispensation at all for the fact that I had just left medical training and was totally green? Did you make *any* sense of it at all?'

'Some. Although there is also a box of memorabilia which you need to sort out. Did you bring your diary with you?'

Kyle patted his jacket pocket. 'I've been reading it on the book tour and trying to join the dots. Not easy. Ruth's diary is going to have to fill in a lot of gaps.'

Lulu stood at head of the table and watched him move down the line, smiling and then more sombre as he picked up one file and then another, before pressing both palms flat against the table and sighing out loud.

'Well, this seemed like a good idea a week ago. I now have ten days to relive all these memories of people and places and create something meaningful. Seeing it all spread out like this makes me realise just what I have got myself into.'

He turned to one side and gave Lulu a short

bow. 'You've done a fantastic job. Truly. I would never have been able to do this in the time. The scope is the problem.'

'May I make a suggestion?'

There was a chuckle from the tall man as he ran both hands back from his forehead through his hair in a totally natural and spontaneous gesture, clearly oblivious to how charming he looked. 'Anything. Please. I'm begging you.'

'It might make sense for you to work through one month at a time. Perhaps take one month a day and write up everything you can think of, based on your notes and the background material. That way you can trigger your own memories about each month you were there.'

Lulu picked up an old airline boarding card and waved it around. 'How did you travel there, for example? Mum took a flight, then drove a truck from the city. Could you use that as a way into the diary? How you felt when you arrived at the camp? What the journey was like? Why you chose to go there in the first place? That's what I would be interested in.'

Kyle looked at her in silence for a few seconds, his brow creased with concentration.

'That…is a brilliant idea. Thank you. It would be an excellent place to start. As to why I went there in the first place…' He started to shake his head with a sigh. 'Well, that is a story in itself. Do you really think the readers would be interested? I had my reasons, but they are personal.'

'Of course,' Lulu replied in a gentle voice. 'And that would be your decision. I did get the impression from Mike that they were looking for that personal touch, but if it is painful…and some of it is bound to be painful…then they have to understand that there are boundaries. I know I couldn't write about—well, how my mother died, for example. I just couldn't.'

Her eyes were so fixed on the rug that she hardly noticed that Kyle had come over to her, until he reached out and took her hand, startling her with the gentleness of his touch.

'And I am an idiot for talking about my pathetic problems when you and your family paid a much greater price. I am sorry for being so insensitive.'

The sincerity and affection in his voice was so overpowering that for once Lulu felt like giving in and confessing everything about her confused emotions.

'No need to apologise. I know how this book ends, remember? But I don't know how it begins.' She smiled back at him now, and broke the tension between them as she slid her hands from between his. 'Are you really a two-finger typist?'

He grinned and wiggled his long, slender fingers in the air. 'I lied. Two fingers each hand. If I take my time and use the delete key a lot. Fear not—I won't be disturbing you or your family with ferocious hammering of the keyboard. Speaking of which—' he looked around the room '—when I do I meet the other Hamiltons? Are they out for the evening, or gone into hiding in fear of the wild man from Nepal?'

'The other Hamiltons?' Lulu asked, confused for a second before she realised what he was saying. 'Oh, you mean the rest of the Hamilton family? Well, you have just met them. Belle is a complete flirt, of course, but she doesn't hog the bathroom or leave her laundry on the floor. We get on very well.'

There was silence for a moment before Kyle replied in a low voice. 'You and Belle? That's it? You live in this big house all on your own?'

There was so much concern in his voice that Lulu frowned before replying. 'Yes, that's right. The Taylor family have lived here for generations. And I have no plans to change that.'

A chiming clock on the mantelpiece sounded out the hour, and Lulu turned to it in disbelief. 'Have you seen the time? I am so rude. You must be exhausted. Shall we meet back here at, say, nine tomorrow? That gives you time to get settled in and decide on how you want to work.'

'Nine would be great. Of course I don't want to disturb the rest of your evening.' He hesitated, then drew a piece of paper and a pen from his pocket. 'I shall need directions to the nearest hotel. Can you recommend some place fairly quiet?' He tapped his pen twice on the pad before frowning, which only seemed to increase the depth of the creases around his eyes. 'The media company have been fantastic, but it would be great to have some time to catch up with my sleep and not worry about waking everyone with my coughing in the night.'

Lulu brought her eyebrows together and stepped closer. 'Coughing? I thought you were taking antibiotics?'

He nodded before replying with a sigh. 'This infection likes me too much. The new drugs are helping, but it's going to take a while. Probably about ten days, actually. Strange coincidence that, isn't it?'

'Um…very,' she replied, with a nod of under-standing. 'And who said doctors make the worst patients?

'Anyway, I thought you would be staying up with the media execs at Lanston Manor.' Lulu raised her nose high in the air and wagged her fingers in the direction of the front door. 'It's about ten miles closer to London and qualifies as our local stately home hotel. Much more suitable for you celebrity authors.'

Kyle snorted, and replied with a belly laugh

that echoed around the quiet high-ceilinged room and was immediately followed by some serious coughing. A dry cough. Rasping, and so alarming that Lulu leant forward in concern as Kyle bent over from the waist for a few seconds before he recovered and pressed one hand to his chest, which he rubbed furiously before shaking his head at her.

'No more jokes like that, please. A stately home? I don't think so. The foundation is paying my hotel bill, not the media people. Every penny I spend on fine dining and fancy beds will be coming out of the Nepal budget. A room above a country pub will be fine.'

Lulu hissed in air between her teeth. 'I see. In that case turn right at the end of the lane and the Feathers is at the end of the village, next to the river. My godmother runs the place and the meals are excellent. But quiet? On a weekend? That could be a problem.'

Kyle nodded and sighed out loud. 'I'm used to late shifts, and it is within walking distance. The Feathers is the place.'

And then he looked straight at her and smiled *that smile*. The kind of smile that bored deep into her body like a laser beam of heat and combustion.

In that life-changing instant her deep frozen heart melted into a pool of warm smooth honey that flowed throughout her body, filling it with the most delicious kind of longing and delight. Fuelled by the presence of this man standing in front of her, her treacherous heart leapt in her chest, yearning, simply yearning for him to touch her and stay with her as long as possible. The sensation felt so sweet and startling that it had to belong to another woman. Not her. Not plain old country girl Lulu Hamilton.

Which was probably why the next words that came out of her mouth were so startling that someone else must have said them.

'There is one other alternative. Would you like to stay here with me? I have plenty of room.'

# CHAPTER SIX

KYLE'S eyes widened and his jaw dropped.

That's incredibly generous of you,' he replied, with a touch of disbelief in his voice, 'but I couldn't possibly stay here. What would your boyfriend say? And then there are the neighbours. Kingsmede strikes me as a very small village. Thank you for the offer, but I think I've already caused enough problems for you.'

And that really did make Lulu stare at him.

The idea was not *so* very ridiculous. They could work more effectively, and the house was large enough that they would not be crowding each other. He was the one who wanted the book completed as fast as possible so he could get back to his life.

And he was worried about *her* reputation?

'Well, someone has a very high opinion of themselves! Prepare yourself for a shock. You are not as irresistible as you seem to think you are. Yes. You.' She pointed with one finger as the totally gorgeous man in front of her dramatically reeled back and pretended to be horrified at the revelation. 'And, just to make it clear, I may not have a boyfriend at the moment, but I do have a self-contained ground-floor studio.' Lulu busied herself with knocking the edges of some paperwork into straight lines so that she would not have to look at Kyle. 'My father had a bathroom installed there when he was ill, and I spend most of my time working in the studio anyway.'

Satisfied that the edges of the folders were aligned in parallel rows, she raised one hand towards the ceiling. 'You would have the whole of the first floor and the family bathroom to yourself. And as for the neighbours…'

She looked up and returned Kyle's gentle smile.

'Fifteen years ago there used to be a stream of medics arriving at all times of the day and night for free board and lodging. Plus, you are helping to build a new unit at the hospice. That gives you quite a few bonus points on the respectability scale; so don't worry about my friends in the village. Unless, of course...'

Her voice faltered, and she tilted her head before giving Kyle a cheeky smile.

'Unless? Please continue. I am finding these revelations so informative.'

'I was just going to say...unless you don't think that you will be able to resist my feminine charms for a whole ten days, Dr Munroe. Is that what you are worried about? Or should I expect your girl-friend to arrive any time soon?'

The smirk on his lips told her everything she needed to know.

'No girlfriend. Or wife. Only the press—who have been following me around like bloodhounds for the last week. *They* might find our arrange-ment a little too cosy to ignore. I can just imagine the headlines.'

'Good point,' she acknowledged. 'Leave that to the Kingsmede Neighbourhood Watch team. They

can be a little over-protective. The press won't
know what's hit them.'

A giggle escaped from Lulu at the thought of
what would happen if city photographers started
digging for saucy gossip about her from the
lunchtime drinkers in the Feathers. Her godmother had been known to twirl a wicked rolling
pin when she had to. Now, *that* would almost be
worth seeing.

Kyle still looked uncomfortable, his knuckles
white as they pressed against the back of a hard
dining chair.

'What do you say, Kyle? Do you want to spend
the foundation's budget on tiny bottles of fancy
shampoo and a gargantuan buffet breakfast? Or
would you like to stay here, where you can enjoy
the peace and quiet you need and risk your saintly
reputation being ruined for ever? I'll even ask
Belle to let you pet her now and again, as part of
your relaxation therapy.'

She paused.

'Unless there is another reason why you don't
want to stay here? I don't like this quiet thing you

do. It worries me. So out with it. I've started to come around to the idea. What's holding you back?'

*What was holding him back?*

The question echoed around the room and re-verberated inside Kyle's mind.

For the last ten years of his life he had pushed himself hard. Very hard. Accepting every mission that Mike Baxter could find, regardless of danger or distance.

Jungle. Desert. High mountain ranges.

Driving himself day after day in a relentless search for something—anything that would prove that he could make a difference to the lives of people whose only hope for healthcare was the foundation.

And he *had* made a difference. He knew that. Time and time again.

So why was it not enough?

In all of those long, exhausting years he had failed to prove to the only person who truly mattered that Ruth Taylor Hamilton had not died that day in vain.

*Himself.*

*He* should have been in the ambulance that morning when Ruth had diverted onto a road set with landmines to avoid an army convoy.

*He* should have died that day. Not Ruth. Not this amazing woman's mother.

And he had been working every hour of every day since to convince himself that fate had not made a terrible mistake.

Except that fate in the form of a publishing contract had decided to play a cruel trick and bring him here. To the last place on the planet that he had ever expected to see. The house and family that Ruth had left behind. So that he could write about the worst—and the best—nine months of his life.

Suddenly aware that he had been staring at his hands, he looked up and locked eyes with this woman he barely knew and who was so full of surprises that he could hardly keep up.

What would she say if she knew the truth?

Would she still be inviting him to stay in her family home?

Or did destiny have another trick up its sleeve?

Was Lulu Hamilton the final piece in the puzzle of how he could finally put the past behind him?

He had never walked away from a challenge in his life.

And yet standing now in this quiet room, looking at the thick woollen socks of a girl who had lost her family, he felt as though he was standing on the edge of a precipice looking out over an unknown land.

A land where his heart was in control of his head.

He lifted his head to gaze in silence at the blonde only a few feet away. Both of her hands were pushed hard down onto slim hips. Several corkscrew curls had escaped from her bandana to create an aura of softness against her pink-flushed cheeks and gleaming eyes.

Blue the colour of a winter sky. Fire and ice.

She looked absolutely mesmerising.

He was going to need a guide before he could hope to venture into territory this dangerous and hope to make it through to the other side.

Her eyebrows came together in fierce concentration when he lifted his head to speak, as though she was willing him to reply with some profound and very logical explanation.

'I do have one question before I make my final decision. What are you planning for dinner this evening at Taylor House?'

'This evening?' Lulu replied casually. 'Oh, the usual. Home-made Shepherd's pie and green beans, followed by local cheese and crackers. All washed down with supermarket red wine.'

His eyes fluttered closed, his chest lifted, and his right hand pressed fervently over the place where his heart should lie as his mouth puckered into a contented smile.

'My private fantasy has come true,' he whispered. 'Miss Hamilton, I would he honoured to be your house guest.'

And then he spoilt the enchanting illusion by stepping back, shrugging the tension from his shoulders and rubbing both hands together briskly.

'How soon can we eat?'

Lulu punched her pillow and turned over in the narrow bed. Then turned over again, twisting her duvet around her body, trying to find a comfy spot. And failing. Tugging the pillow over her head in disgust, she was forced to finally admit defeat and throw off the overheated covers.

Even her normally faithful Belle had tired of the constant tossing and turning and headed off to find a quieter spot at some point during the night.

She had slept in the studio many times and never had any trouble getting off to sleep before. What was the matter with her? Or should that be *who* was the matter?

The very idea that a man like Kyle Munroe was sleeping in her spare bedroom only a few yards above her head was enough to keep her head spinning.

How did he do it?

Was this normal?

Did he create chaos and upset wherever he went, like some smiling and benevolent tornado? Because he had certainly worked his magic in this house.

Had she been secretly sending out some kind of subtle message that said, *Please come into my*

*home, which I have been guarding against in-
truders for the past ten years, and why not bring
my pain from the past along with you? And if you
wouldn't mind paying me some attention while
you are, that would be nice too.*

What had she been thinking?

Sitting at the dinner table the previous evening
he had been the perfect house guest, filling her
kitchen with laughter and funny stories about his
life in Nepal while he relished every mouthful of
her food. It had been a pleasure to share his plans
for the clinic, fired by his passion for his work and
for people he lived with.

Perhaps that was why her dreams had been filled
with soft-focus images of the cover photograph of
Kyle from his first book blended with the real-live
Kyle who had sat on her kitchen floor to play with
Belle while she washed the plates?

Of course he was fascinating.

Of course he was handsome and charming and
totally worthy of any schoolgirl crush.

Of course she wanted to get to know him better.

And of course her foolish heart should listen to

her head. In ten days the cough that had interrupted their meal more than once would be gone, Kyle would be on a flight back to Kathmandu, and the tornado would have moved on, leaving her to clear up the devastation left in its wake.

Throwing her pillow onto the floor in disgust, Lulu slid her legs off the bed and opened her eyes a crack. Early-morning daylight filled the open-plan studio through a gap in the fabric blinds covering the floor-to-ceiling windows.

She sauntered down the hallway to the kitchen, stretching her arms above her head. And stopped, frozen. The kitchen light was on. Lulu swallowed down a fleeting thought of burglars before sighing out loud.

Her house guest. Of course. Kyle must be an early riser.

Groaning inwardly, because she was not prepared to speak to the live version of the man from her dreams, Lulu lifted her chin, inhaled deeply, and strolled into her kitchen as casually as she could.

It was empty, but the back door was slightly

ajar, and she stepped outside. Kyle was standing on her patio in bare feet, stretching his right arm high above his head, then his left arm, turning his neck from side as a gentle cough racked his ribcage. He was oblivious to the fact that as he did so the crumpled T-shirt he was wearing had risen up above the waistband of a pair of bottom-hugging jeans, exposing a healthy expanse of tight abdominal muscles.

Lulu had never appreciated the full meaning of the term *'six pack'* before that moment, and it was going to be a long time before she forgot it.

Bells, whistles and several years' worth of unused female hormones sounded off inside her body, and she would have been quite happy standing there for a lot longer with a smirk on her face. The damp, cold morning was a blessing for her burning neck and cheeks. He was edible. Top to toe.

Except that out of the corner of her eyes she saw a red setter come hurtling around the corner of the house, and within seconds her delicious treat was ruined as the dog jumped up into Kyle's arms and was twirled up into the air, barking and barking in delight as he scrubbed her fur with his hands.

Lulu's heart melted.

*He liked Belle. And Belle adored him.* She was doomed.

Then Kyle turned around and saw her.

She could only gawp at the tousle-haired man as his eyes widened and shifted a little lower, before he twisted his mouth as though he was biting the inside of his cheek.

Lulu glanced down at what she was wearing and raced back inside the kitchen, her face burning again—now with embarrassment. Flowery flannel capri-length pyjama bottoms combined with a spaghetti strap top which barely covered her chest might be suitable for Belle—but for male house guests? In cold weather?

She had a sudden vision of what she must look like and almost squealed in horror.

Luckily her fleece jacket was hanging behind the door, and she quickly shrugged it on before turning back to face Kyle with a fixed smile as he threw a dog toy for Belle.

'Good morning. Did you sleep well?'

The Greek god covered a yawn with one hand, and then ran his fingers through what passed on him for bed hair. Totally relaxed.

'And good morning to you. I hope I didn't wake you up with my coughing? I had forgotten how hard it is to sneak downstairs in old houses with creaky floorboards.'

'I didn't hear a thing,' she replied truthfully. *Especially since she had not fitted her hearing aid yet.* 'Was Belle a pest?'

'Not at all. She was excellent company.'

It was only when he shuffled into a chair and dropped his head back, eyes closed, that Lulu noticed the dark shadows and pale skin and gasped.

'Have you been up all night?'

He gave her a wry smile as a reply. 'Not *all* night. I managed a few hours' sleep.' He must have noticed the concern in her voice. 'Kingsmede must be having a calming influence on me. I usually get by on a lot less. Why are you shaking your head like that?'

'I distinctly recall Mike Baxter telling you to rest.'

'Advising me to rest,' he replied, then startled her by reaching out and running his long slender fingers through her hair. She froze, unable to move and frightened to speak, until Kyle held up a long white feather with two fingers and waved it in front of her face. 'I think your pillow has sprung a leak.'

She smiled back, the tension broken. 'Old pillow. Old feathers. Thank you.'

'No problem,' he murmured. 'I am available for any kind of personal grooming duty you might have in mind for the next ten days. Just snap your fingers and I'll be there.' And with that he clicked his thumb and third finger together and locked eyes with her at the same time. 'Especially if you wear your hair like that.'

Her hand instinctively moved towards her head, which was a mess of unruly damp-frizzed curls, but he clasped hold of it instead and ran his thumb along the back of her knuckles.

'Don't change a thing.'

Then, releasing her hand, he pushed himself to his feet before she could reply.

'Since you made dinner yesterday, the least I

can do is prepare your breakfast. I can see buttered toast and marmalade on the horizon. All you have to is sit where you are, looking gorgeous.' At this point he waggled his eyebrows a couple of times. 'And help me with the one question that has kept me awake in the night.'

Lulu took a breath. A twister had truly hit her little house in Kansas. 'Well, put like that, how can I resist? What would you like to know?'

Kyle had turned to the refrigerator, and she had to strain to hear what he said, but the words penetrated her heart and mind like a bullet.

'You've read your mother's diary and her letters. What did she say about me?'

Lulu sat stunned for a few seconds, and waited until Kyle was cutting bread before focusing on what he was saying.

'Please don't think I'm arrogant, but studying has always come easily to me. Perhaps too easily in many ways. Medical school was hard, but I never felt challenged. When the chance came to go and work for the foundation I thought I was going to change the world. One country at a time.'

He waved the breadknife in her direction, as though conducting an orchestra. 'Yes, I know. Young and foolish. Green as grass. All of my life to that point I had been told how clever and gifted I was. And here was my chance to do some good with all of that talent.'

Butter and preserves appeared on the table, then Kyle pressed both palms flat on the pine surface. 'I was an idiot. And it took Uganda to prove just how wrong I was. About everything.' A wry smile creased his mouth. 'I've just spent an hour reading through the records from my first month at the mission, and I am totally embarrassed by how unprepared I was. Ruth and the rest of the crew made sure that the patients didn't suffer, but looking back now it must have been a lot of extra work for them, with precious little gain.'

Lulu tried to focus on the movement of his hands as they set the table, willing him to continue, delaying the inevitable. She dared not look into his face.

'I'm not going to hide any of this. If the media

company expect this book to be all about how great I was, then they are going to be disappointed.'

Lulu looked up in concern. 'You are going ahead with the project, aren't you? I've already told the hospice that they can expect a donation.'

His hand stilled, and he stared down at her with pain in his eyes, brows twisted together as he replied in a low voice, 'Of course I'm going ahead with it. I made a commitment to my clinic, the foundation and your charity. I keep my promises. I'll finish the book—it's up to them whether they publish it or not. But it would make a difference if I thought Ruth believed that I had achieved something worthwhile by the end of those nine months.'

She breathed out a sigh of relief as he offered her a plate of crisp toast, but did not speak until he had taken a bite from a thickly buttered and marmaladed heavy crust. Watching his face contort with the simple pleasure of good food made her words seem foolish and pathetic.

'I wish I could answer your question, but there is a problem.' She waited until he was chewing before picking up her own piece of toast. 'You see, I have never read anything she sent home during the last year of her life. Not one word. So I have no clue what she thought about you. Or me. Can you pass the marmalade, please?'

His face paled and his toast hit the plate.

'Please tell me that the papers are not burnt or lost somewhere,' he said, in a decidedly less confident voice.

She shook her head. 'All the documents that came back from the mission are on the table in the dining room. I'm talking about the private letters and diaries. My dad kept everything safe while I was at university. They're all here, bundled up inside an old suitcase in my dad's studio.'

Kyle breathed out loudly, then stared at her. Hard.

'And you have never read them?'

'No.' She swallowed down her toast with a slug of hot tea. 'It was simply too painful after she died, and my dad never discussed it. He knew that I wasn't ready.'

Kyle sat back in his chair and nodded slowly. 'I can understand that. Are you ready now? I *would* like to see her diaries, but it has to be your decision.'

*I don't know. And I don't want to read any of it, but I know that I have to.* 'As far as I know the diaries from her previous missions had a lot more to do with the day-to-day running of the clinics. That's where we need to start.'

'Are you okay with that?'

Lulu lifted her head and sniffed. She had known this moment was coming for the last week. No surprise. She simply had to face it and do the job she had promised. That was all.

'Yes. Those diaries will be fine. In fact, I can go back to the studio right now and find them for you.'

It was as though Kyle sensed that she had made her decision and they were back on track, and his mood seemed to lift immediately.

'Your studio? Ah. The Kingsmede centre of the art forgery trade.'

'Shush! I thought you said that your lips were sealed.'

She shot him a wide grin, and all the sunlight he had ever wanted was back in the room. Grey gone. This was what he needed. Wanted. This ray of sunshine. Perhaps that was why he heard himself saying, 'I've never been to an artist's studio. Do you mind if I make yours the first?'

Her mouth opened, then closed, before she answered him with a faint smile. 'If you like. There is not much to see at the moment. Come this way.'

Kyle glanced at Lulu as they strolled along the wide staircase side by side. She was clearly oblivious to how tantalising a prospect it was for any man to be walking behind her, and he decided to enjoy the moment for as long as possible.

She glanced sideways at him, as though a hidden sensor had detected that she was being ogled. 'Before I forget, you can look forward to restaurant food for dinner tonight. My godmother has organised a welcoming committee in your honour at the Feathers this evening.'

'Excellent. I look forward to meeting your friends.'

'Before you get too comfortable, I should give you advance warning that Emma is responsible for raising funds for the hospice. I'm sure some cunning scheme has already been launched to make the best use of you while you are staying in Kingsmede. A naked doctors calendar, perhaps? The topless fire crew were very popular last year!'

She stopped outside what looked like a bedroom door and leant closer. 'Prepare to be dazzled.'

Without waiting for an answer, Lulu gently turned the brass handle, casually swung open the wooden door and stepped through.

It was the complete opposite of what he had been expecting.

Instead of the chaotic blend of startling bright colours that decorated the rest of the house, the walls and ceiling of this space were painted in a brilliant white. Light flooded in from the plain glass windows illuminating one single picture hanging over a large white fireplace. It was a life-size portrait of Ruth Taylor Hamilton, and it was so life-like that the impact of seeing her again knocked Kyle physically backwards.

He was so stunned that it took a few seconds for him to notice that Lulu had already started rummaging around inside a tall cupboard.

'Was this where your father worked?' Kyle

asked, gasping in a long breath. He pressed both of his palms flat against the wall behind him, so that he could take in the entire space and regain his control.

'This was his studio for as long as I can remember. I used to play on a battered old sofa that was in the corner there, whilst he painted. In the winter we would light the fire and make toast whenever we felt like it. And sometimes we'd paint together, or just chat. This was always a happy room. He loved working here.'

'You must really miss him.'

Lulu looked into Kyle's face. 'I do. I know it sounds ridiculous, but after he died I used to come in here almost every day and just smell the paints. I only needed a whiff of linseed oil to bring him back to me. There are so many good memories of this place. I had some magical childhood moments here.'

Kyle Munroe moved closer to gaze at Ruth's portrait for a moment, hands on his hips before leaning forward and staring more closely at the signature.

'T. D. Hamilton? Is that your dad?' he asked, his voice low and business-like.

Lulu came and stood next to him, smiling up at the brightly coloured acrylic portrait of a very pretty young woman dressed in white against a landscape of blues and greens.

Her mother's energy beamed out from the canvas, her warm smile captured for eternity.

'He rarely did portraits. My mum was the exception.' She looked across at him and was surprised to find him still staring at the picture. 'Do you like it?'

He nodded. 'Very much. It's so lifelike. Ruth was a lot older when I met her for the first time, but there is no mistaking who it is.' He paused and turned towards her, so that they were only inches apart. 'There is a lot of love in that painting. He must have been extremely talented. Again, I am very sorry for your loss.'

Lulu looked into his face and saw something so intense that it took her breath away. A raw pain that brought tears pricking into her eyes. Just when she'd thought she had no more tears left to give.

'Are you also thinking of someone close? Lakshmi—that was her name, wasn't it?' she asked, her voice calm, low, as objective as she could make it.

He moved forward and gently wiped away the tear from her cheek.

His fingertips felt textured and rough on her skin. A soft smile lit his face from within. 'It was. But there have been so many. Friends who went to climb mountains and never came back. People I tried to help and couldn't. I get to know my patients as well as any doctor. It always hurts when you get there too late to make a difference—when clean water and a few simple medicines would have...' He swallowed hard. 'You are very intuitive, young lady.'

Then the moment was lost, and the big boyish grin came back like a mask and he closed down.

'You never forget them, you know. The patients who don't make it.' He shook his head. 'Far too many.' And with a final glance at Ruth's portrait, he squeezed Lulu's hand tight before turning to stroll out of the room.

'Kyle. Wait a moment.'

He whirled around to turn back into the room—only she walked faster and their bodies collided softly, surely, linking together so naturally that they seemed destined to be together.

It was pure reaction that drew his hands tight around her waist to steady her—but pure attraction that held them there for a lot longer than necessary. The only thing that he could concentrate on was the depth of the ice blue of her wide eyes and the gentle rise and fall of her chest against his shirt as their breathing became heavier. Hotter. He could have stayed there a lot longer, fuelled by his need to be close to this amazing woman, but Belle started barking outside, and in that instant he glanced over at the portrait over the fireplace.

*Ruth.* And Lulu was her daughter. What was he doing?

Instantly he relaxed his grip.

'Steady, there. Why did you want me to wait?'

Lulu swallowed down the trembling dizziness that was rapidly taking her down the road to heartbreak. This was only their second day together, and Kyle was already turning out to be far more of a temptation than she ever could have predicted.

Every time he touched her it was becoming more and more difficult to look away and remind herself that he was only here to work. That was all. Except that if she had stayed in his arms one more second there was a very strong possibility that she would have wrapped her arms around his neck and done something very foolish.

And very regrettable.

'The suitcase is on the top shelf. Could you lift it down for me, please? It is rather heavy.' She pointed to the tall cupboard, delighted to have something to distract her from the bulk of him standing so close that she could smell the tang of his body. 'Then it's time to get back to the toast. You're going to need a lot more carbohydrate before you start reading all that.'

Kyle did not hesitate. 'And coffee. *Lots of coffee*. Now, tell me more about the Feathers. What exactly should I expect this evening?'

# CHAPTER SEVEN

'I THINK you might have warned me that the entire village were going to turn out to see me last night! The children were a riot.'

'Not the *entire* village,' Lulu replied, as she waved to the occupants of a car as they hooted their way past them down the lane leading from Kingsmede towards Emma's cottage. 'Some of the babies stayed home with their fathers. You have to admit that the junior school had done a wonderful job with the welcome banner over the entrance. And the photographs should go very well with the question-and-answer session you gave in the bar. Especially that one with Emma's nieces in it.'

Much to Belle's disgust, Lulu stopped walking, leant closer, and brushed her hand over a stain on

Kyle's jacket. 'I did tell you that Pip and Katy were high on cake and ice cream *before* you hoisted Pip onto your shoulders. I'm sure Emma can get that out.'

'No problem. I did notice one thing in the bar last night.' He pushed both hands deeper into his trouser pockets. 'Everyone I spoke to wanted to know about my clinic in Nepal, and how I was going to raise this money for the hospice, while you stayed in the background. Seeing as you are the reason I am in this village, I'm surprised that Emma didn't make *you* stand on the bar as the star of the show. Any explanation for that?'

Lulu shook her head. 'She knows that I don't like being the centre of attention. That's all. And of course they now have a new celebrity—you were a great hit! And it was your first public outing. They will soon get used to you.'

'I'm not so sure about that. The personal tour of the hotel and restaurant was brilliant. The book signing I could understand. But the autograph hunters? They were…different.'

'Ah…' Lulu hissed, drawing air through her

teeth. 'The Bennett sisters. They run the news-agent and sweet shop on the main street. I admit they were a little over-enthusiastic about their new line in celebrity autographs, but when you reach their age any excitement in the village is welcome. Although, to be fair, it was *your* idea to offer to give them each a personal medical exam before you left town.'

Kyle shook his head with a sigh. 'I only want to make sure that your friends know how hard you've been working on this book. That's all.'

'Thank you for that, but I'm fine.' She paused and stared ahead before she spoke again, in a clear, confident voice. 'I know who I am, Kyle. I have done since I was sixteen. I live my life the way I want to and I'm quite happy to stay in the background.'

He turned and looked at her in silence—really looked at her, as though weighing something up in his mind. Then he startled her by presenting his strapped arm while keeping a tight control of Belle with the other.

'May I have the pleasure of escorting you to the

home of Mrs Carmichael on this pleasant after-noon, Miss Hamilton?'

Lulu opened her mouth to give him a snarky reply, glanced at the half-smile on his face, and hesitated for a few seconds before nodding and threading her free hand through the crook of his arm. 'How gallant, Dr Munroe.' She looked up at the sky, where faint sunlight was trying to break through the heavy grey clouds. 'That would be splendid. If you can take the gossip, so can I.'

'Great. Because the cat is well and truly out of the bag. Your secret identity as an orchid painter has been revealed to the world. Forger or not, now you can tell me the truth about that painting you were struggling with in London that day. I want to know all about life as a famous artist.'

And with that he started strolling contentedly down the lane, under the shade of the great beech trees, with Lulu by his side, leaning into his shoulder.

'Famous artist?' She laughed. 'If only that were true and I had the income to show for it. The gallery owner on the South Bank was at art school in London with my dad, and he knows that I love painting flowers. Especially wild flowers.' She stopped walking, pulled back on his arm and gestured to the roadside, where a tiny clump of bright red flowers was almost hidden in the grass.

'Wild red poppies. They look wonderful with Herb Robert—those pink flowers higher up on the bank. Or even pink blackberry blossom and red rosehips.'

She leant in again as they continued walking and Belle became impatient to get going. 'Of course it is autumn now, so I have to rely on photographs that I took in the springtime. Primroses, daffodils. Wonderful spring flowers. I just adore them.'

There was so much joy and pleasure in her voice that it was infectious, and Kyle could only chuckle in reply as he pretended to scan the bushes. 'I don't see any wild yellow orchids! Can you point them out to me?'

She laughed out loud. 'Not down this particular lane.' Then she play-thumped him in the arm. 'It was a commission from a client who wanted a particular shade of yellow. A one-off. My usual work is a lot smaller and more detailed.'

'Why small? Why not just paint the flowers larger?'

'Because I paint life-size. That's why. No delusion. And here we are.'

Kyle felt her slide her arm from his, and the loss had already hit him before she bent down to pet Belle.

'Now, be a good girl for Uncle Kyle. Aunty Emma does not want you in the cottage—you're far too big and boisterous. And make sure that Uncle Kyle tells you a nice story all about his time in sunny Africa. See you back at the house.'

With one final finger wave she took a firmer grip on her cake box and strolled towards the small row of thatched cottages where Emma lived, leaving Kyle holding a dog lead attached to a mad beast who had just spotted ducks on the other side of the river.

Kyle Munroe sauntered slowly down the wet muddy footpath which ran along the riverbank, heading downstream away from Kingsmede, while Belle scampered on ahead. The light drizzle had turned into heavy rain and they were both drenched.

Which was not such a good idea with a chest infection. Right on cue, he choked on that dry cough he had learned to live with over the last few weeks.

Time to face up to his current dilemma. He was going to have to make a decision soon about the last chapter of the book.

The more he came to know Lulu, the more he realised that the pain of the truth would be one more thing for her to carry.

And *he* would be the one piling on the burden. How could he do it? How could he add to her problems? That would be the exact opposite of what he intended. He should be doing everything he could to make life easier for her.

Lulu was not only Ruth's daughter, but also a very special person, with an approach to life he had never seen before. Grounded, certainly. But something else. Something that had intrigued him from the first day when he saw her on that tube train. Lulu possessed an inner serenity, a self-contained calmness which acted like a lure. Drawing him to her.

In a few quiet moments last night in the Feathers, he had noticed the way she smiled at everyone she met without any hint of pretension or false emotion.

This was Lulu with the people who knew and cared about her as a valued member of their extended family, and she clearly cared about them in turn. Was it the village? Or was it Lulu herself?

Kyle looked around him at the picture-postcard thatched cottages that lined the footpath opposite the river. Their lovely gardens were bursting with late roses and apple trees heavy with fruit. Kingsmede and Lulu would always be linked together in his mind—she was just as much part of this village as the square-shaped ancient stone church, the Feathers and the winding river.

Perhaps Lulu's inner peace came from knowing who she was and where she wanted to be? Her sense of place. Was that it? It would certainly explain why he was lacking that perspective on his own life.

An hour later, just as Kyle was about to turn

back towards the village, he glanced up and saw the very woman he had been thinking about walking towards him—only this time in heavy weather gear, carrying a golf umbrella.

He started jogging towards her, whistling for Belle as he did so.

She gingerly stepped towards him with a smile.

'Everything okay? I thought you were with Emma?' Kyle spoke calmly, matter of fact, trying desperately to suppress his concern.

She shook her head. 'We are both fine. It's you I'm worried about. I have an extra waterproof here for you, and warm gloves. This rain is getting heavier, and I have no intention of completing your book on my own. You, sir, are soaked.'

With that she pulled a long parka from her bag and passed it to Kyle, who thanked her and shrugged it on over his head.

She looked around. 'What have you done with my foolish dog? Has she run back home on her own without you?'

'Drat—she was here a second ago. You go that way. Meet back here in a few minutes.'

Lulu walked as fast as she could in the pouring rain, but it still took five minutes to reach the footpath that ran down the length of the river.

And there was Belle.

The ducks had been nesting on an island in the middle of the river that was swollen from weeks of autumn rain. The foolish dog had started swimming out to them, barking, only to find that the downstream current was too strong for her.

Lulu watched in absolute horror, calling Belle's name, as her dog was slowly carried down the river by the power of the water. She was a strong dog, but inexperienced. The river widened in a few yards, and would probably be shallow enough for Belle to stand up in as long as she didn't panic.

But, to her horror, Belle started barking, out of control, and fought the current—which meant that she was swimming away from the shallows and into the fast-flowing deep water.

Lulu started to jog along the riverbank, calling to Belle to come to her. Come to the bank and be safe. Belle had been her constant companion

since her father died. Nothing could happen to
Belle. It simply couldn't. Even the thought of it
was starting to give her palpitations.

Suddenly the ducks and swans lifted from the
river, and Lulu turned to see what the problem was.

Kyle had started wading out into the water, and
the fast-flowing river was already up to his thighs.

Without discussion or argument, Kyle simply
crouched down in the water and waited until Belle
had been carried to him by the current. He grasped
her around the middle and hoisted the sodden
animal over his right shoulder into a fireman's lift.
His arm held on tight to her scrabbling legs as she
wriggled like a fish from the waist.

Slowly, slowly, so as not to drop his precious
cargo, Kyle turned around in the river and waded
through the water and onto the riverbank.

'Oh, thank goodness. Are you both okay?'
Lulu managed to get out, as Kyle bent his knees
and allowed Belle to take her weight on her
own feet as she slid from his shoulder. Lulu
wrapped her arms around Belle, then repeated
the process with Kyle.

They were rewarded by a full-body shower as Belle tried to shake herself dry.

'Oh, thanks a lot. Ingrate. Come on you two. *Home.*'

Lulu wandered back into her kitchen, where Kyle was stretched out, half-perched on a kitchen chair, back against the wall, sipping a steaming beaker of tea. His hair was still tousled from the rough drying it had received from the kitchen towel.

'She'll be fine now. Dry, clean and happy. Let that be a warning to us all about the dangers of chasing ducks across a fast flowing river.'

Kyle snorted. 'Looked to me like she was having the time of her life.'

Lulu grinned back, and fluttered his eyelashes at him. 'She was, but thank you all the same. Belle means a lot to me. You are officially our hero. There may be a medal.'

'I don't feel like much of a hero.'

'This is a small village. Standards are low. We'll take what we can get.'

Kyle saluted her with his drink. 'Faint praise,

but I will accept it nevertheless. What made you decide to come looking for us?'

Lulu sat down opposite him. 'Emma and I were concerned when the rain started to get heavier.' She raised both hands in surrender. 'I know that you are the medic around here, but your coughing seems to have improved over these last few days. Of course that was *before* you decided to take a swim in the river . The future of Kingsmede as a spa town depends on your good recovery.'

'Well, I would hate to let the tourist trade down. Did Emma enjoy her cake?'

Lulu sniggered her reply. 'Loved it. Especially the sickly sweet icing, bursting with artificial colours. All washed down with *two* glasses of pink champagne.'

'Is it her birthday?'

'Not exactly. Long story.'

He cocked his head to one side. 'I have nothing else to do this evening except relive trauma in the African bush while Belle is snoring in front of the fire.'

'True.' Lulu sat down opposite Kyle. 'Have you ever heard of the Memory Book Project? It's one of the techniques they use at the hospice, and Emma asked me to help with hers. Basically the person creates a record of the life they have lived, their family history and customs, who their friends and relatives are. Anything they want their family to remember about them when they are gone.'

She smiled up at Kyle, and was humbled by the look of admiration on his face.

'Our generation is used to technology. Photographs, videos, digital images. Not so ladies like Emma. Photographs were expensive before the war. So these memory books can take their place.'

'So, *have* you helped Emma with her memory book?'

Lulu nodded. 'I made some copies of the only photograph Emma has left from her wedding. It was taken outside Kingsmede church. And she started telling me about her wedding day.'

There was a pause as Lulu looked out of her

kitchen window at the lashing rain. 'It was a warm sunny morning. The whole family were walking back to the cottage where she still lives today for the wedding breakfast, and they had just reached the river when her new husband, Frank, slipped off his smart shoes and waded into the water with her in his arms, twirling her around and around, laughing and laughing, until they were both dizzy—with happiness and love. So much love.'

Lulu felt tears pricking at the corners of her eyes.

'He died of a brain haemorrhage. He was her soul-mate. Her one and only. They would have been married fifty years today.' She smiled across at Kyle, only he was focusing on the table, his brows tight with concentration.

'And I am babbling. Sorry.'

'You're not babbling. I'm so sorry for Emma's loss. She's a wonderful lady and deserves your love. What's more, you have just given me a clue to what I've been looking for!'

He clutched hold of her fingers, eyes bright, shining with energy and excitement.

'What you are talking about is a kind of scrap-book. A collection of pictures, thoughts, memories. Snapshots from the past that come together to make a complete story. Is that how you see it?'

Lulu simply nodded, bowled over by the change in Kyle. He was transformed. 'Yes. That's exactly right.'

'*That* is how my poor medical brain works. I see those separate parts, but I have a problem putting them all together in a long piece of writing. What if I write the book in that way? Memories. Maps. Photographs. All the separate pieces. I can do that, and I would enjoy it. What do you think? Would it work?'

She blew out, and made the mistake of looking at him—and was instantly swept away with his new-found passion and enthusiasm. A picture began to form in her artist's mind's-eye. 'A bright African collage. Oh, yes, I think it would work. It would work very well.'

'It's brilliant! You are brilliant.' And before Lulu knew what was happening Kyle had leant forward and kissed her heartily on the cheek as he clasped a tighter hold of her hands in his.

She pulled back her hands and smiled, trying to break the tension, but then moved back to rub Kyle's hand.

'Your hand is freezing! How stupid of me. You need a hot shower. I would never forgive myself if you caught a cold. Come on—off with your wet clothes.'

She was rewarded by the kind of seductive grin most girls would melt for.

It worked.

'Well, that's the best offer I've had all day.'

'It's the one and only offer you're going to *get* all day. Here. Let me help you.'

Even with Lulu's help it took five minutes to peel off Kyle's jacket and sweater over the strapping on his left wrist. He was drenched, and Lulu could see him shivering despite her central heating.

She grabbed a thick bath towel and came back into the room just as his shirt hit the floor. She leered, and despite her best intentions she lusted. Then lusted a lot more.

Kyle Munroe had the chest, shoulders and arms of a male model.

Not an ounce of spare flesh covered the well-defined body.

Lulu enjoyed a few more minutes of pleasure as he bent to remove his boots and socks, stretching the spectacular muscles across his broad shoulders, revealing an amazing expanse of taut, smooth skin with a covering of dark hair that was tantalising even before she noticed the waistband of his black underwear.

The reality of his work and life were only too evident from the sharp division lines between the dark brown of his lower arms and neck and the faint tan on the rest of his upper body. He looked as though he had plunged his head and arms into brown dye, and Lulu could not resist laughing out loud at the thought, helping to break up the sensual awkwardness of their situation.

'Well, *someone* has been working out!'

Kyle flexed his right bicep and heaved his boot to his chest in a joky demonstration of his weight-lifting skills, before lowering it back to the tiles.

'You need upper-body strength for the ice climbing. Not that I've done much of that recently. I've been way too busy at the clinic.'

Lulu gasped with horror as she gently touched one finger to the end of a jagged scar that ran over one shoulder and down his back. Smaller white lines were scattered across both of his arms, and across the bicep of his right.

'Is that what climbing does for you?'

He sniffed, not wanting to break her touch on his sensitive exposed skin. The delicious sensation of that single light fingertip had already set his heart racing and his body pulsing.

'A lifetime of accidents. Usually in the middle of nowhere. Pakistan—now, that was remote. When you have to stitch up your own skin one-handed, you can bet money the wound will be somewhere it's hard to reach.'

'Do you really expect me to believe that?' She looked at Kyle for a moment before exhaling loudly. 'You're *not* joking. Madness!' And then she looked at his strapped wrist. 'Can you manage in the shower?'

She was rewarded by a huge grin. 'Exactly what kind of service are you offering, Miss Hamilton? Do artists receive special training to help in shower emergencies?'

'I was thinking of turning the water on for you, Dr Munroe, and finding you a plastic bag to cover your strapping. Possibly even finding you an extra towel. But of course that would be far too comfortable for a macho hero such as yourself.'

He looked around the room in pretend amazement. 'What did I say?'

'Had your chance. Blew it.' She pointed to the stairs. 'Shower! I'll get your wet clothes into the washing machine, and hope they don't disintegrate with the shock of hot water and detergent.'

'Can you use extra fabric softener?' Kyle asked in a pleading voice. 'I have such sensitive skin.'

Twenty minutes later Kyle walked into the dining room looking far better than any man had the right to, and Lulu's poor treacherous heart performed a double somersault with a twist.

She still had not recovered from the topless incident.

Vigorous use of the coal scuttle and log basket had created a pathetic excuse for her overheated cheeks and burning neck, and the open fire was already burning bright in the fading light, its orange-and-white flames licking up the chimney, creating shadows around the room. A single lamp glowed gently in the corner, and Lulu could hear the sharp crackling from her seasoned apple and beechwood logs.

It was the hair, of course. Any man would look edible with that length of tousled please-run-your-fingers-through-me curly hair. She could offer him a comb, but on second thoughts she decided she liked him just the way he was. Delicious.

He caught her staring, and glanced down at his clothing with a quizzical look, stroking the fine fabric of his Italian sweater. 'Will I pass?'

'For the moment. Perfect timing. The hot chocolate is almost ready. And help yourself to cookies.'

Kyle bent down to scratch Belle's head a couple of times, before collapsing down onto the sofa, his legs stretched out towards the open fire—where Belle had already dragged her fleecy bed before settling in for a snooze.

'That's better. I feel almost human again, and a lot warmer. That fire is gorgeous. Come and sit next to me and talk about Kingsmede. Anything you like. Tell me more about you and Emma.'

Lulu smiled as he patted the sofa cushion next to him and raised his eyebrows. She filled two beakers with hot chocolate from a saucepan on the hearth, and perched on the end of the sofa as far away from him as possible.

'As you wish, great hero! You drink. I talk. Deal? Was that a nod? Emma is so much more than my godmother. She gave me a refuge when I needed one. And then she gave me a job and a career! How about that for starters?'

'I need lots more details. Please carry on.'

'Okay. You already know that she has always lived in the village. She was born here. Emma knows everybody.'

Kyle blew on his steaming beaker to cool it marginally before taking a sip. 'So you were actually born here, as well—in Kingsmede? Mmm. This is good. Cinnamon?'

He took another sip as Lulu nodded. 'Cinnamon and a pinch of chilli. And, yes. Apart from a brief spell at university, I have lived in this village all of my life.'

'Wow! I didn't think that was possible any more. I have no idea how many flats and houses I lived in with my folks.'

Kyle frowned, as though trying to estimate how many homes he had used as a hotel over the years, before catching Lulu's eye.

'Please carry on. Emma has lived here all of her life. Got it. What happened to make her your refuge?'

'What happened was the annual arrival of the homeless and usually penniless waifs and strays from whichever far-off land my mother happened to be working in at that time. "Oh, just turn up," she would offer. "Tom will give you a warm welcome and somewhere to stay. Plenty of room in Taylor House."'

Lulu stopped, and realised that she had been gesticulating with her spoon.

'And so they came. Sometimes we picked them up from the airport; sometimes the docks. And still they came. At first it was the occasional nurse or medic who needed somewhere to rest and recuperate before going to see their family or start their next assignment. Then a few families started to appear. Perhaps a woman and a child who we had to take straight to the nearest hospital. Later whole families. Trying to escape a war zone.'

She stopped as Kyle sipped, his attention totally focused on her face.

'You know what's it like to arrive in a strange country where you don't know the culture. Often you can't speak the language, and the weather is something like today. Or colder.' She shook her head. 'The words *culture shock* do not even come close. But we managed. There was always something we could do, and they truly *did* need our help. And sometimes they carried letters home from remote clinics.'

'So what went wrong?' Kyle asked, still totally focused on her.

'Drink up!' she said, then she nodded. 'Yes, it did go wrong. I remember having a bad day at school. I was studying hard for my exams. Oh, I loved school, but I had been teased. Again. I just wanted to go home and cry. Only when I got home…'

'You found a house full of strangers?' Kyle filled in the gap.

'The crying and yelling was so loud that I had to shout to ask where my dad was. I followed the loudest of the screaming to my own bedroom, where my dad was sharing out my clothes to the children who were running around him, throwing all my precious books and clothes around the room. My project work for school had been torn and trodden on.'

There was a pause as Lulu played with her cookie.

'I was seventeen years old, and suddenly, at that second, I just stood there, with the chaos and noise all around me, and realised that I wanted a normal life. With two parents and a home I could call my own.'

Lulu's voice dropped an octave as she brushed crumbs from her trousers.

'I know that sounds incredibly selfish, but I just picked up my books and stuffed them into my school rucksack, with the few clothes that I had left, and walked to Emma's cottage.'

Lulu brought the plate of cookies to the sofa, so that Kyle could finish them off, and sat down next to him, her legs under her, both hands wrapped around her beaker.

'I slept there every night for the next fourteen months. In exchange I worked in the hotel kitchens and learnt how to prepare accounts. Oh, I came here to the house every day, and checked that there was food in the cupboards and that the bills were paid and all the practical stuff. I didn't just leave Dad to cope on his own. Then I went to London to art college for a while. Apart from that, I lived with Emma.'

'What changed? What made you go back home? Did he start turning folk away?'

'Oh, no, he would never have done that. Never.'

Lulu sat back against the cushions and suddenly felt queasy at the smell of the hot milk.

'Lulu?'

'My mother died. But you already know all about that.'

She suddenly found the contents of her beaker quite fascinating.

'How did you find out? Did someone phone?'

'Mike Baxter came to see me at the college. All he could tell me was that her ambulance hit a land mine.' She looked up. 'He told me that it would have been very quick, but I always wondered how accurate he was about that.'

Kyle reached out and meshed the fingers of her left hand with his chocolate-smeared long fingers.

'It *was* instant. I'm so sorry—it must have been very hard to hear like that.'

Lulu sat up straight and took a breath. 'I moved back the day after Mike came to see me. As for Emma... She had a blood-pressure problem last year, but the Emma you saw in the Feathers is not so different from the Emma she has always been.'

'Then I'm glad to have met her. Do you miss them? Your parents?'

Lulu paused for a moment, before swinging out her legs.

'I think I've talked far too much for one afternoon. Now, we really should get back to work. At the moment I am up to month four, and things are not going too well....'

Then Kyle's hand was on her waist, the gentle pressure turning her towards him and closer, ever closer, so that they were looking at one other on the sofa, their faces only inches apart. His hand moved to her cheek, his thumb on her jaw as his eyes scanned her face back and forth.

'Don't lock me out. Please.' His voice was low, steady. 'Trust me, Lulu. Can you do that? Trust me?'

# CHAPTER EIGHT

BEFORE she could answer, his hand moved to cup her chin, lifting it so that she looked into his eyes as he slowly moved his warm thumb over her soft lips. Side to side. No pressure. Just heat.

She felt his breathing grow heavier, hotter, and her own eyes started to close as she luxuriated in his touch.

Then he snatched his hand away to cover his mouth as a dry cough shook his upper body.

'Sorry. I think I swallowed some of your Kingsmede river water,' he gasped in a hoarse voice. 'Complete with duck feathers.'

He slid to the edge of the sofa and stretched up before reaching for his boots. 'Do you mind working later? Your wonderful crazy hound just cost me five hours.'

Lulu hissed at him as Belle lifted her head and thumped her tail hard against the floor, before settling down again, nose on paws in her comfy dog bed.

'Perhaps you should take the rest of the evening off? Being a hero must be *so* exhausting!'

There was a long sigh before Kyle replied. 'True. We *are* ahead of schedule, and I need to call my family some time today.'

'*Family* business? Now you really *do* have me intrigued.' Lulu rummaged around on the coffee table until she found a familiar book with a distinctive cover, and she waved it in front of Kyle's face before he had a chance to reply.

'I liked your book. But I do remember thinking that there were a few things missing. No mates, no ex-girlfriends—not even an anxious mum waiting at home.' She laughed. 'She must be very proud of what you have achieved.'

She looked up at his face and was taken aback

by the sadness he displayed for a few seconds, before the smiling grin went back on.

Lulu broke the silence, her voice low to disguise her thumping heart.

'Sorry. I didn't mean to pry. It really is none of my business. Besides, you might spoil the surprise for the next book, when all will be revealed!'

Kyle answered by reaching out and taking Lulu's hand in his, startling her. He slowly splayed out each finger as she tried to clench her hand into a fist, and stared down at her palm.

'Long lifeline.' He looked up into her eyes. 'No, Lulu. I didn't leave a broken-hearted mother back in London. In fact, it was more like the other way around. She broke mine. As for girlfriends? Well, nothing serious.'

She didn't dare to breathe or speak at the sadness and regret in this precious man's voice. A sadness that almost overwhelmed her—a sadness that made her want to wrap her arms around him and share every ounce of heat in her body.

'After my parents' divorce my mother remarried and moved to Australia with her new family. There was nothing for me there. I'd finished medical school here in England, so I took off to the most remote part of the world I could find.'

His eyes moved up to hers just long enough to check for understanding.

'Yes. I ran away to Africa to escape my parents' messy divorce. As for being proud of me? Well, I don't know about that. I get the occasional letter, and I know she's read the book. Maybe I'll ask her that question next time I see her?' He beamed a smile out to her. 'That should get the conversation off to a flying start.'

'When did you last meet up in person?'

'In the departure lounge of Singapore Airport,' Kyle whispered. 'About a month before her first minor stroke. She moved back to London soon afterwards with my half-brother, Alex, to start a new life as a twice-divorced woman. The second stroke was two weeks ago.'

Lulu took a sharp intake of breath. 'A stroke? Oh, Kyle. How is she?'

He smiled across at her. 'Recovering. Mother made it clear to Alex that she didn't want me to see her until she had better control of her speech and hand movements. Luckily for me, my half-brother is not someone who follows the rules, and he has been keeping me up to date. She should be discharged from hospital next week.'

'I hope it goes well for you,' Lulu replied, with a sincere sigh of regret.

'Do you believe that there is one person for each of us in this life, Lulu? One soul-mate, like for your Emma? My mother is already on her second divorce. It doesn't bode well for me.'

She looked into his face and saw something she had never seen before. Serious, yes. Concerned, yes. But more. This was fear.

Kyle was looking at her, holding her hand as though his very life depended on it. The flippant answer she had ready died on her lips, and she hesitated before speaking, her fingers moving to mesh with Kyle's, bonding them together.

'Yes, I do believe that. I have seen it.'

He lifted one hand and pushed her hair back from her forehead. 'I have no regrets. Once an adrenaline junkie, always an adrenaline junkie.'

Lulu looked up and raised her eyebrows, let him continue.

Kyle stopped and reached out for the copy of *Medicine Man* Lulu had left on the table.

'Do you see that photograph on the cover? I remember it like yesterday. The biting cold. Brilliant sunshine. I can still smell the smoke from the Buddhist offering to keep us safe on the mountain!' He looked up at Lulu and grinned. 'Those sorts of memories have to be earned. You can't buy them or trade them. You just have to be there, at that moment in time and space. That's special.'

Lulu found something fascinating in the bottom of her cup, then whipped around to face Kyle, her voice trembling.

'I've never understood it. *Never.* People in Kingsmede think that I've somehow come to terms with the danger of what my mother did for a living, but they are so wrong. If it was just adrenaline you wanted there are roller coasters, or any number of things that have thrills. Without the risk of killing yourself. And yet you still chose to climb mountains—by the most dangerous route, no doubt.'

She stretched out her hand towards Kyle as he started to shuffle closer.

'Your parents are probably just grateful that you lived this long and they still have you with them—even if it is for only a few weeks between missions. Sometimes family does have to come first. So don't expect the rest of us to feel grateful that you've lowered yourself to join our mundane existence. And—'

Before Lulu realised what was happening, he had wrapped his hand around the back of her neck, his fingers working into her hair as he pressed his mouth against hers, pushing open her full lips, moving back and forth, his breath fast and heavy on her face.

His mouth was tender—gentle, but firm. As though he was holding back the floodgates of a passion which was on the verge of breaking through and overwhelming them both.

She felt that potential, trembled at the thought of it, and at that moment she knew that she wanted it as much as he did.

Her eyes closed as she wrapped her arms around his back and leant into the kiss, kissing him back, revelling in the sensual heat of Kyle's body as it pressed against hers. Closer, closer, until his arms were taking the weight of her body, enclosing her in his loving sweet embrace. The pure physicality of the man was almost overpowering. The movement of his muscular body pressed against her combined with the heavenly scent that she now knew was unique to him alone and filled her senses with an intensity that she had never felt in the embrace of any other man in her life. He was totally overwhelming. Intoxicating. And totally, totally delicious.

Then, just when Lulu thought that there could be nothing more pleasurable in this world, his kiss deepened. It was as though he wanted to take everything that she was able to give him, and without a second of doubt she surrendered to the hot spice of the taste of his mouth and tongue. Cinnamon and chocolate. And Kyle.

This was the kind of kiss she had never known. The connection between them was part of it, but this went beyond friendship and common interests. This was a kiss to signal the start of something new. The kind of kiss where each of them were opening up their most intimate secrets and deepest feelings for the other person.

The heat, the intensity and the desire of this man were all there, exposed for her to see, when she eventually opened her eyes and broke the connection. Shuddering. Trembling.

He pulled away, the faint stubble on his chin grazing across her mouth as he lifted his face to kiss her eyes, brow and temple.

It took a second before she felt able to open her eyes—only to find Kyle was still looking at her, his forehead still pressed against hers. A smile warmed his face as he moved his hand down to stroke her cheek.

He knew. He knew the effect that his kiss was having on her body. Had to. Her face burned with the heat coming from the point of contact between them. His own heart was racing, just as hers was.

'Is that the way you usually silence women who ask you tough questions?' Lulu asked, trying to keep her voice casual and light as she tried to catch her breath. And failed.

He simply smiled a little wider in reply, one side of his mouth turning up more than the other before he answered in a low whisper, 'I save it for emergencies. And for when I need to know the answer to an important question.'

'Hmm?' He was nuzzling the side of her head now, his lips moving over her brow and into her hair as she spoke. 'Important question?'

Kyle pulled back and looked at her, eye to eye. 'I had to find out if you were holding on to a secret unrequited love. Now I know the answer I can do something about it. So. Would you care to risk being seen out in public again with me?'

Lulu leant back and took another breath, before grinning at Kyle. 'Well, I might.'

He bowed in her direction and pressed his fore-finger onto his lips, as though considering his options. 'I happen to know that the Feathers has roast chicken on the menu this evening.' He dropped his hand and pushed it deep into the pocket of her father's best trousers. 'Would you care to join me for dinner, Miss Hamilton? No strings. Or do I have to use my emergency procedure again?'

'Dinner? That's it?' Lulu answered, knowing perfectly well that it was not the only thing he was offering.

'What do you think?' He winked.

And then she made the fatal mistake of looking into those eyes and was lost.

The words that came out of her mouth seemed to have no connection at all with the intentions of her brain. And everything to do with the desire burning in her heart.

'Thank you. I would love to have an evening out. In fact, I was wondering if you would like to be my guest at Emma's birthday party next week,' she said, giving him a polite smile, as though he had not just completely rocked her world. 'We always hold it here, and I'm in need of an escort. Since I'm between boyfriends at the moment, I suppose that you will have to do. If you're available?'

'An escort? Well, how could I resist such a tantalising invitation? I'm available. Assuming that nobody better comes along in the meantime, I presume?'

'Oh, yes.' She nodded and pursed her lips. 'I'd drop you straight away. But don't worry. I could probably pass you off to the Bennett sisters. They don't mind sharing.' A smile widened her mouth. 'I can be ready in ten minutes.'

A few minutes later Kyle was standing in the hallway in his coat, wondering how he'd got there and if he had truly just kissed Lulu Hamilton. Or had he merely dreamed that part of the last hour?

He had not planned to kiss her. Far from it. But the energy and passion of that woman was a flame, and he was the moth.

If ever he had lived for the moment, that had been it.

And, despite everything she had said, and the hurt he had unwittingly caused, when she'd kissed him back the intensity of the woman had made his heart soar.

She had pressed buttons in his body which had not been pressed for quite some time. The sweetness and intensity of that brief kiss had left him reeling—but his brain was still working.

This was no one-night stand. It was too deep, too special. Like her.

She had just told him what she thought about men like him—men who lived for the moment, not caring for the consequences. He had even admitted it himself.

It was true. He knew it, she knew it—and there was precious little he was going to be able to do to change her mind about that.

And yet…she had managed to do something he would have thought impossible. For the first time in years he was actually thinking about having something more. He *wanted* to try and convince her to give him a chance to prove that he was different. That he was going to be the exception to the others. That he would not break her heart when he took off to pastures new. That he was worth her time. Her affection. Her love, even?

And perhaps convince himself at the same time.

It was time to take another of those insane risks.

And take an evening off. In the company of the only woman he wanted to be with.

Kyle stamped his feet on the welcome mat before strolling into the warm, bright and welcoming kitchen, still redolent of the breakfast bacon and tomato sandwiches he had shared with Lulu over several pots of tea while looking at the amazing party invitations Emma had sent out for her birthday celebration that evening.

They had laughed until they'd cried before setting to work for a few hours.

The memory book idea was working. Pictures, memories, facts and extracts from letters and diaries seemed to come together like magic to recreate a real place and time.

The book was going to be everything he wanted it to be and more. It would be a superb tribute to Ruth and the entire team he had worked with all those years ago.

And he could not have done it without Lulu.

The irony of that fact was starting to worry him more than a little. He had just spent the last-half hour by the riverbank, trying to work through the dilemma that would have to be decided in the next few days.

How was he going to end his book? With the truth? Or with the tributes and press statements the foundation had issued? Mike had no idea that there were two versions of the series of events. How could he? The only other person who knew was a paramedic working in Uganda who had probably forgotten all about it.

The more he worked with Lulu, laughed with Lulu, shared his life with Lulu, the more he wanted to be completely open and honest with her—just as she had been with him. She deserved to hear the truth from him, irrespective of whether he wrote about it in the book or not. No more lies and deception. Not with Lulu.

He cared about her far too much for that. Only if he was going to do it, it had better be soon— or not at all. And that was the problem.

Could he risk the relationship they had already built up? He knew that she cared about him. Would the truth destroy any chance they might have of taking things to the next level? Because one thing was for certain. Against the odds, he was falling for Lulu Hamilton.

Belle scampered up to his side with a gentle huff of a woof, as if to say *home at last*, her nails clattering on the polished floorboards either side of the rug before she attacked her food.

A delicious smell of hot coffee and burning logs wafted into the hallway as Kyle slowly raised himself on tiptoe and peeked into the dining room. Not that anyone would have heard him above the din of pop music bellowing out from the open door.

Lulu was standing on the top rung of a tall stepladder, apparently oblivious to the decibel level. Her hips were gently moving from side to side in line with her shoulders, and she was totally ignoring the swaying of the ladder and the impending doom which might accompany stretching upwards towards a high ceiling with both hands full of tools.

Lulu hummed along to the pop music blasting out from her sound system as she tightened the drill bit with her chuck key. The hammer drill made short work of the brick and plaster, and the plug fitted perfectly. Seconds later the picture hanging screw was in the wall and secure. She stepped down one rung on the ladder to measure the drop from the intricate plaster moulding of the dining room cornice. Exactly the same as the first. Excellent.

The pictures had been crooked for years. It was time.

Lulu was just about to move when she felt something touch the bare section of skin between her jeans and the bottom of her old T-shirt. It was icy cold, and running up and down her ribcage, and it was trying to tickle her under her arms. She squealed out loud.

As she whipped around in shock her left hand grabbed the ladder. At exactly the same time the heavy drill in her right hand swung around with the momentum of the movement. And made contact with Kyle Munroe's head.

'Ouch!' Kyle staggered back to sit on the sofa in a heap.

'Oh, no! I am *so* sorry.'

Lulu scrambled down the ladder and stood next to him as he clutched his head.

'I had no idea you were there.'

'My own fault for creeping up on unsuspecting females, I suppose. I did call out, by the way, but I can see now why you didn't hear me.' He pointed towards the drill, then to the sound system, where loud music was still belting out into the room. 'Having the music that loud can damage your hearing, you know.'

'Oh, really? Thanks for the advice. So can sneaking up on people.'

She moved her hands from her hips to look more closely at the side of his head, where he was rubbing vigorously. She started to reach forward to touch his hair, and pulled back, cautious. 'No sign of blood. How are you feeling?'

'I'll live. And I am the medic around here,' he mumbled under his breath as she tidied away the tools.

'I thought you would be out most of the morning. My dad used to say that a straight picture was a boring one. I don't think my party guests would agree. Sorry again.'

'No problem.' He chuckled. 'Belle disgraced herself with your local swans. They were not impressed, and...Lulu?'

No reaction. Strange. Unless... He snapped his fingers over to his left. Still no reaction.

Her hair was pulled back into a scrunched-up ponytail, and she was wearing her old working clothes again, but she somehow managed to look in control, calm and absolutely stunning. Her inner serenity shone out.

Kyle walked slowly over to Lulu's right side and helped her coil the drill cable before pulling a slip of paper out of his shirt pocket. 'I come with a message from the lovely Emma. The good news is that she has found the curtains you were looking for.' He raised his eyebrows high and gave her a quizzical look before going on. 'The bad news is that they have run out of lemon drizzle cake at the Feathers. So you will have to make do with chocolate muffins.'

'Well, she might have warned me.' Lulu paused.

'How can I possibly hang pictures, fit curtains or type without lemon cake?'

She glanced up and caught him staring at the left hand side of her face, where her hair was barely covering her ears.

*He knew.*

She smiled and held out the sides of her overalls to create a skirt before bobbing him a short curtsey.

'Ah. You've noticed that I have a hearing problem. Well, I am impressed. Most people take a lot longer. So now you know. Stay on my right side and you'll be fine. Stay on my left and you can say whatever you like. There's a good chance I won't hear half of it.'

'Have you always had a problem in that ear?' Kyle asked, his eyes focused on her, intensely interested.

She paused just long enough for him to know that this was not something she talked about very often before she smiled up.

'It might surprise you to know that I have actually been to Africa. My dad and I visited Mum in the summer holiday I turned sixteen. She managed to get a few days' break on the coast at some medical conference or other, and we had a great time.'

Lulu busied herself unpacking Kyle's dictation machine, her head down.

'I came home with a very interesting souvenir—or at least that's what the tropical disease hospital in London called it. Encephalitis? Meningitis? They never did find out exactly what it was. But I was dosed with every antibiotic they could find, plus a few more experimental ones. I recovered with my brain intact and most of my organs doing what they were supposed to. Except one ear. So overall I would say I was very lucky.'

Kyle whistled and shook his head at her calm and matter-of-fact reply. 'I would say you were very, *very* lucky. Your parents must have been terrified.'

Lulu unwrapped the delicious-looking chocolate muffins before answering in a low voice. 'I was too far out of it to notice what was going on, but according to Emma my dad was hysterical.'

Lulu paused and looked up at Kyle with a smile.

'He actually sent a message to my mum and asked her to come home. Now, that was serious. He had never done that before.'

'Did Ruth come home?'

Lulu shook her head. 'There was no point. By the time the message reached the field station I was in recovery. She called from the nearest large town about four days later. I don't know what she said to him, but I know that was my one and only exotic holiday. Shame, really, but there was nothing else he could do. Fact.'

She passed the muffins across the table towards Kyle, skirting the plastic wallets of diary notes. 'I suppose you are well used to those sort of risks?'

He nibbled into the chocolate icing and tried hard to deflect the question. 'Mmm, this is good. And I seem to recall that it was your hearing that we were talking about. Does it still cause you a problem?'

She laughed and shook her head. 'You don't want to hear about that. Far too boring. And I know you have too much to do to chat to me.'

He held up his right hand. 'On the contrary. I

do want to know. The work can wait a few minutes. Please. I'm interested.'

Lulu shuffled the paperwork a few seconds longer, but when she spoke, her voice was lower, calmer, slower.

'Okay. I'll start with a question. When you go climbing in the mountains, do you ever stop in the middle of nowhere and just listen? And marvel that you cannot hear anything manmade? Just the sound of the wind, probably your own breathing. No planes. No cars. No radios or anything else from the modern world.'

Kyle nodded, not willing to break the fragile connection held in her voice. 'It's a very special moment.'

Lulu rearranged the folders in front of her. 'That is what I miss. I miss the sound of silence. And, yes, I have been to specialists in hospitals all over the country, and tried the latest digital aids. They have no idea what caused it, or how to stop the tinnitus I get now and again. So I've learnt to compensate. But I'll probably never hear the sound of silence again.'

She smiled at him with the kind of tilted head, crinkly smile that melted his heart. 'On the plus side, my right ear is fine—so I still hear birds and ocean waves. Telephones. I love listening to music, and if I listen really hard and overcome my fear of calling attention to myself I can still hear a lot of what people say. Even if it is only one or two at a time.'

She glanced away to look out of the long windows at the open fields which stretched beyond the trees. 'So, yes, I would say that it *does* bother me. But it could have been a lot worse. I almost didn't make it.'

Kyle started to rise from his chair—only Lulu whipped back to face him so quickly that he caught her off balance, and he had to grab her around the waist and pull her towards him to steady her.

Lulu pushed down on his shoulders to steady herself, and made the mistake of looking into his face. And was lost, drowning in the deep pools of his eyes which seemed to magically bind her so tight that resistance was futile. She tried to focus on the tanned creased forehead above the mouth that was soft and wide.

Lush.

He already had the slightest hint of stubble at noon, so the rest of his body must be… No, she couldn't think about what was below the chest hairs curling out from the V of his shirt.

Sitting in her chair, she could see his head and throat were only inches from her face. Her bosom was pressed against the fine fabric of his sky-blue shirt. In a fraction of a second Lulu was conscious that his hand had taken a firmer grip around her waist, moving over her old overall as though it was the finest lingerie, so that she could sense the heat of his fingertips on her warm skin below.

She felt something connect in her gut, took a deep breath, and watched words form in that amazing mouth.

'I think we make our own destiny…' Kyle tried to join words together in a sensible sentence.

He gave up, because Lulu had slowly closed the gap between their bodies, drawn towards him by invisible ropes of steel.

'Destiny…?' she whispered.

'Who dares wins. Don't you take chances, Lulu?'

'Only with you…' Lulu replied, but the words were driven from her mind as Kyle's fingers wound up into her hair. Drawing her closer, he slanted his head so that his warm, soft lips gently glided over hers, then firmer, hotter.

# CHAPTER NINE

THE sensation blew away any vague idea that might have been forming in her head that she could resist this man for one second longer. Her eyes closed as heat rushed from her toes to the tips of her ears and everything else in the world was lost in giddy sensation.

She wanted the earth to stop spinning, so that this moment could last for ever.

Before she could change her mind, Lulu Hamilton closed her eyes and kissed Kyle Munroe back, tasting the heat of his mouth, breathing in the heady smell of coffee, chocolate crumbs and a musky aftershave, sensing his resistance melt as he moved deeper into the kiss.

Her own arms lifted to wrap around his neck.

She let the pressure of his lips and the scent and sensation of his body against hers warm every cell in her being before she finally pulled her head back.

Kyle looked up at her with those wonderful hazel eyes, his chest responding to his faster breathing, and whispered, 'Here's to taking chances,' before sliding his hand down the whole length of her back and onto her waist, drawing her forward as he moved his head to her neck and throat, kissing her on the collarbone, then in the warm hollow below her ears, his fingers moving in wide circles around her back.

'Oops. Perhaps those curtains can wait.'

Lulu opened her eyes in time to see the back of Emma's coat, and in one single movement she pulled back and smoothed down her overall with one hand as she gathered up her hair which had mysteriously become untied with the other.

'I…er…need to check on a painting. A present. For your mother.' Lulu just about managed to stammer out, and waved her hand towards the hallway. 'Painting. Studio.'

Kyle nodded. 'Great idea. Me too. Photos. Yes, photos. Catch up with you later. Right. Later.'

'Okay, this is new!' Emma stood at the end of Lulu's bed with her arms folded.

'Yes,' Lulu said, still feeling slightly giddy. 'It was a moment of reckless madness. He made the move and I decided to go along with it.'

Emma breathed out with a shake of her head. 'Oh, Lulu. I can see that he is very good-looking, but Kyle is a tourist. He will be gone in a few days. Are you ready for that?'

'Yes. I know,' Lulu said. 'If only he wasn't so amazing.' She closed her eyes and tried to recreate the heat of his mouth, his fingers running up and down her spine, and could not resist grinning like a fool.

'Well,' Emma said, 'you are old enough to make your own decisions, young lady, and if he makes you happy, good luck to you both. In the meantime, I have a party in a few hours. See you later.'

Lulu slid down the duvet and pulled the pillow over her head. She groaned out loud. Emma was only repeating what she already knew in her head. She did know the risks—better than most people.

It would probably be a lot easier if she didn't need him so badly.

Kyle leant back in the hard chair at the dining table, opened a computer file, and tried to focus on his memories of a distant place in a country he had last visited ten years earlier. Pity that all he could think about was Lulu.

He hadn't planned to kiss her, touch her.

She had kissed him back.

Where had that come from?

His eyes squeezed tight with frustration. *When had he become such an idiot? Just who was he trying to protect here?*

Lulu knew the score, and had been honest with him from day one. If anyone was being selfish, it certainly wasn't Lulu.

In a few short days Lulu had become his closest friend—the person he wanted to be with. Laugh with. Confide in. He had told her things about his past that not even his family would know about until they read the book. How had that happened?

Idiot.

Except that when he touched her face… Wow. Lulu was…so right. Beautiful. Hot.

And a lot more than that.

She had invaded his dreams day and night. Dreams of a life away from the stress and pain of the work he had chosen. Work where his only goal was to make a difference to other people's lives. Not his own. That was the legacy that Ruth Taylor Hamilton had left him, and he had to live up to that. Only now Ruth had given him something more—something so precious he was almost afraid to grasp hold of it, in case it fractured like a thin piece of crystal glass between his fingers.

So where did that leave him now?

This was Ruth Taylor Hamilton's daughter. He should go to her right now, tell her about her mother and take the consequences.

Big mistake. He needed to sort this out and do it now. Because what he was feeling was something new. And more terrifying than facing the highest mountain.

Yet he knew in his heart that this was one risk that he needed to take or die trying. Because he would never have this chance again.

His cellphone rang and Kyle casually flipped it open, his mind full of possibilities.

'Kyle Munroe,' he said, and then closed his eyes. 'Alex?'

His half-brother. The man he had only met once in his life.

'Hi, Alex. Sorry to sound so slow. I'm just in the middle of something. Thanks for getting back to me. Please go ahead.' He picked up a pen and started tapping it onto the smooth surface of the table before writing down an address. 'She'll be ready to be discharged from hospital next week? Fantastic. Yes, that would be great. Early afternoon would be fine.'

Kyle lowered the pen and pressed his forefinger and thumb hard into his forehead in fierce concentration before speaking again.

'No. I told you that I would respect her wishes.

I'll make sure that I keep out of sight until you tell me she is ready to see me. Okay. See you then. Thanks, mate. Thanks for your help.'

With a great sigh, he leant back and closed his eyes. His mother was going to make a good recovery. That was one more thing to be thankful for.

Kyle was so preoccupied with dates and timings that he barely noticed that someone had come into the dining room and was talking to him.

'Hello, Kyle. Want to keep an old lady company for a few minutes?' Emma laughed and pointed to the window seat. 'It would make my day!'

Kyle leant forward and grinned. 'Show me an old lady and I'll answer your question.'

He raised his eyebrows a couple of times before giving her a suggestive wink.

That really got Emma going, her shoulders moving up and down with laughter as she wriggled down in the cushions. She waved a finger at Kyle as he positioned himself so that he was facing her.

'Lulu warned me about you, young man. You

can save your charm for my only goddaughter. Although…'

'Although?' Kyle repeated, cocking his head to one side.

'I'm pleased that you are working on this book together.' Emma nodded her head. 'Ruth was a good friend to me over the years. She would have been proud of Lulu and what she has achieved. Yes, very proud. You will be working for a very good cause.'

'So you've known the Taylor and Hamilton families a long time?'

Emma narrowed her eyes and looked hard at Kyle. 'I was born in this village. Spent my life here. There aren't many folk I don't know one way or another. But why do you want to know?'

Kyle looked into Emma's face and recognised that she wanted a real answer. 'Well, for one thing, I admired Ruth Taylor Hamilton a very great deal. To do her memory justice, I'd like to know more about the lady before she became a pioneering surgeon.'

Emma sat back in silence, clearly sizing Kyle up.

'I knew Ruth very well. Eccentric, you might

say, but bright! Sharp as a knife! And driven. I don't need to tell you that war surgeons like Ruth were not doing it for the wages.'

Kyle nodded. 'Well, that hasn't changed.'

She cocked her head to one side and stared at Kyle through narrow eyes.

'You married, handsome boy? Engaged?'

Kyle drew back and gave Emma a look.

'Me? No, Emma. Nobody is daft enough to have me. Or should that be brave enough?'

Emma blew out a puff of air. 'Daft. Courage is only part of it.'

She leant forward and grabbed Kyle by his right shoulder, looked into his face.

'Want some advice from someone old enough to be your grandmother? Because you are going to get it whether you like it or not. Don't leave the people you love to face the loneliness Tom and Lulu Hamilton had to look forward to every day. Stay single. Although…' she patted his face before sitting back '…there might be a few broken hearts along the way, a good-looking boy like you. Am I right?'

'Not too many, I hope.' He sat back, slightly stunned by the intensity of her words, and fought to change the subject. 'How about you, Emma? From what I see at the Feathers, there is a lot of mischief going on in a village this size.'

She smiled. 'I was lucky. I had some wonderful years. Sometimes it seems like yesterday.'

She looked down, her eyes glistening. 'It doesn't happen like that twice. Now, get yourself to that studio and talk to Lulu. I need my beauty sleep before the party. Remember to save a dance for me.'

'Wouldn't miss it for the world.'


Lulu pulled open the blinds on the studio windows and was dazzled by the sunlight flooding into the long, narrow room. Slipping off her shoes, Lulu slid down the wall to sit cross-legged, facing the windows.

She was exhausted.

Lulu brought her fists down onto her knees. Hard. *Stupid! Stupid girl!*

Had she not learnt anything?

How was Kyle any different from any of the

other handsome young medics who had stayed in this house for a few days or even weeks over the years, until boredom set in, the next job came along and they were gone as fast as their legs could carry them?

Every one hooked on the rush. The adrenaline. The excitement. The thrill of exotic locations and hardship.

So what if he is gorgeous looking, charming and caring? When did that become so unusual?

She was stupid to think he was any different from the others.

Stupid to think he was special.

She took a breath. Stupid to think that he might actually come to care about her. Love her. Want to share his life with her.

Lulu dropped her head as tears pricked the corners of her eyes, burning.

Stupid to think that she could trust him to want to be with her instead of his work.

To dream for just a moment that he would come home and live in this village. Come back and stay.

Her parents had loved each other. But it had not

been enough to make her mother want to stay. Ruth Taylor Hamilton had abandoned her husband, just as she had left her daughter behind to face her loneliness.

A tear rolled down her cheek and Lulu choked back others. She had always promised herself she would not cry about things she could not control. And now look at her.

Kyle stood transfixed and gazed in wonder as Lulu dropped her head back against the white walls of the artist's studio, her joy and serene calm acting like a spotlight, so that the entire room seemed to come to life when she was in it. How could he ever get tired of looking at her?

This was the image he would have to store away for those days when the satellite phone and the webcam failed and he was down to a photo—an imprint of a cheeky smile and those stunning whirls of long, blond, corkscrew curls. But all he wanted to do now was throw his rucksack into a corner of this room and tell her that he was not going anywhere. And keep on telling her, over and over again, until she finally believed him.

Perhaps then, at last, she would trust him enough to let him into her heart.

Except of course he might not be able to keep that promise. The TV company had planned to film in Uganda for a week. Fly in, fly out. But he knew precisely what would happen. A few days into the clinic and he would be stuck there until another medic could take over. Where would that leave Lulu?

What could he offer her? A short-term affair would be wonderful, amazing and unforgettable. But then what? A tearful farewell at some airport and six months of misery, during which he would work himself senseless every day to block out the loss?

While Lulu got on with her life in Kingsmede. Alone again, deserted by yet another medic on a mission.

Kyle looked away as he saw her mouth twist into her tears, torn between wanting to be with her and wanting to quell the fire in his belly he felt whenever they were in touching distance.

Emma Carmichael knew what she was talking about. He had a choice to make. Stay single and go back to the work that had been his refuge for the last ten years. Or change his life and find a new direction which was even more terrifying and uncertain.

Because one thing was clear.

He was infatuated with Lulu Hamilton and there was not a thing he could do about it. There was one task, however, he *could* help her with.

Lulu quickly swallowed down her tears when the door opened a little wider and she looked up to see Kyle standing there, leaning against the doorframe, filling the space.

He looked so handsome he must belong to another woman, another country and another life. He could not possibly want to be hers. She had been kidding herself with a silly teenage crush. How pathetic was that?

He shuffled down next to her, so that he could wrap his arm around her shoulders.

Lulu closed her eyes for a second, to luxuriate in the sensation of his hair and his stubbly chin on her skin. The smell of a citrus shampoo. His smell.

She could not help but instinctively snuggle closer, so that she could lean against him as he stretched out his long legs and crossed his ankles.

He drew a folder of papers onto her lap, and the air between them seemed to freeze. It was the folder of her mother's letters and personal documents from the suitcase, which Kyle had put to one side as they went through her diaries.

His arm tightened around her shoulder and his lips pressed against the top of her head.

'I want to thank you for showing me the diaries. You were right—they *were* full of technical details about the mission, but also I found what I was looking for. Apparently Ruth thought that I was doing okay. And that means a lot.'

'I'm pleased,' she managed to squeeze out through a tight throat.

'Now it's your turn to look at some photographs and choose some for the book. It's time.'

She swallowed down hard in pain, aware of his hot breath on the side of her face.

'I'll be right here next to you. We can go through them together. Okay? Here goes.'

And without another word, Kyle turned the package upside down so that the contents spilled out onto their laps.

She could only watch as he casually started rummaging through the jumble of envelopes, single sheets of paper, and something she had not expected.

Her mother had taken photographs. Lots of photographs.

And not just of the stunning countryside and the animals, but of the field hospital itself, and the patients she had treated. In many cases the name of the person had been written on the back, making them even more personal. Smiling men, women and children, some of them clearly very ill or wounded.

And of course she had taken photos of the people he worked with. Paramedics, orderlies, nurses whose names she recognised. There was one of a younger version of Kyle in a white coat, inside a fabric tent. She looked at it for a few seconds before passing it to him with a smile. 'This would be perfect.'

He smiled back and nodded. 'Book cover perfect.' And then he looked down and picked up another. 'How about this for the dedication page?'

It was her mother. The mission leader.

Lulu took the simple crinkly print from his fingers. Centre stage was Ruth Taylor Hamilton, walking with grinning children along a dusty dirt road below a clear blue sky. She was laughing, and she looked so happy as her arms swung wide to lift one of the children up from the ground.

Tears pricked the back of Lulu's eyes and she wiped them away, aware of Kyle's gentle touch.

'I'm sorry this is so hard for you. I truly am.'

Lulu shook her head as she ran her fingertip across the image. 'You don't understand. I'm not crying for Mum. I'm crying because I am so pathetic. Don't you see? I'm jealous. I keep thinking that it should have been *me* in that photograph. *I* should have been the little girl with her, playing and laughing and enjoying life. *I* was her daughter—not these children.'

Her shoulders were heaving with the pain in her chest.

'Can you understand how guilty that makes me feel? How pathetic? These children had suffered so much; they deserved some happiness. I have no right to be envious of that. None at all.'

He was holding her in his arms now, pressing her closer and closer to his chest, drawing her to him. 'Yes, you do. You wanted your mother and she wasn't here for you when you needed her. You deserved happiness as much as they did, Lulu. But you have the rest of your life to look forward to now. And quite a few letters to read. You can do it. I know that you can.'

'Don't do this, Kyle. Please. Don't make this worse than it is.' The quiver in her voice betrayed her and she was forced to stop. To gulp down her panic.

'It's going to be all right now.' His voice was low. Caring. Concerned. Everything she wanted but knew she could never have.

'And, in case you're wondering, you don't get rid of me that easily. Not a chance. You had better get used to that idea. So, now we're clear about that, I would like to hear what's on your mind,

Lulu. Tell me why you were crying when I came in. Is it me? Have I been an idiot?'

Lulu tried to shake her head, but found Kyle in the way.

'No. No, it is not you. You have always made it clear that you want to go back to Nepal as soon as you can. Your work is important there. They need you.' Her head dropped forward a little. 'I knew that from day one. I'm the one who made the mistake of hoping that I might change your mind, Kyle. I'm the one who is being ridiculous.'

Lulu lifted Kyle's arm from around her shoulder and turned to face him. Their noses were only inches apart. She placed one of her hands on each side of his face and her eyes looked deep into forest pools reflecting every shade of amber and green as she forced him to look at her.

'I love my life and my work here in the village. I want to share that life with someone special. But that person has to want to be here. It's totally unfair for me to expect that from you. I am selfish. I know that. I want to wake up with the same person every morning. In the same bed. That's why I wanted you to leave, Kyle. Before…'

Kyle leant his head forward so that their brows were touching. 'Before?'

She smiled. 'I was going to say before we make promises and commitments we want to keep but know in ourselves that we can't.'

There was a huge sigh from the man whose lips were moving across her temple. He slowly pulled away and brought his hand up to push back the wisps of hair which had fallen onto her brow. His fingers stroked through the tight curls, revelling in the unique sensation.

'Is this what the quiet life does? Puts a wise head on such pretty young shoulders? In Nepal you would be called a shaman—a *jhankri*. A witch doctor. Someone who is not afraid to recognise the truth, even when it is hard to hear. But even witch doctors can only heal other people, Lulu. Not themselves.'

Kyle stopped messing with her hair and brought his hand down to cup her cheek as he looked into her face.

'Not many people have come to know me like you do. Know me from the inside. Not even my own family. That is a rare gift.'

Her face creased into a wide grin before her head dropped. 'You're so easy to like.' *So easy to love.* She had to change the subject—quick. 'Now that I've chosen your photos, here's something I painted which *your* mother might like as a present.'

Her fingers creased around the edges of a watercolour sketch of spring flowers that looked so lifelike to Kyle he could almost smell their sweet fragrance lifting from the heavy cream paper.

Her forefinger stroked the edge of the paper, and when Lulu spoke her voice was low and sad. 'Dad never liked my flower paintings. They were too small and too commercial for his taste. Not the kind of work a real artist would do. That's why he wanted me to go to art college. So that I could learn to be a true painter and put this amateur stuff behind me.'

'You really mean that, don't you?' Kyle shook his head in amazement. 'You are so talented, and it's obvious that you love what you do. This is wonderful work, and I know my mother would treasure an original painting like this. You're a very special person, Lulu Hamilton.' He touched her forehead with his. 'So very special. And so beautiful.'

'Kyle? About earlier…'

The telephone rang in the hall.

'It's okay. I have an answer-machine.'

'*What* about earlier?' Kyle mumbled. He was caressing her face now, moving down to her neck, nudging open her blouse with his chin, trying to distract her from listening to the telephone—only to hear Emma's voice echo across the empty space.

'Hi, Lulu. Just to let you know that the party goodies should be with you in about half an hour. See you soon!'

'Half an hour!' Lulu shouted in horror, trying to wriggle herself free from Kyle's grip.

'Relax, sweetheart. You would be amazed at what we can get done in half an hour.'

'Did you just call me sweetheart?' Lulu's eyes widened like a schoolgirl's as Kyle nodded, his eyes never breaking their hold on hers. 'You did?'

'I'll call you sweetheart as many times as you like if it makes you look happy. And you *do* look happy. I can only hope I have played some small part in that.'

'Idiot. You have shown me what happiness feels like—I could get addicted to it. Addicted to *you*. Do you have a cure for that, Dr Munroe?'

He answered by kissing her forehead and neck. Luxuriating in the touch of her skin on his. 'And what if I'm addicted to you? Have you thought of that? A pair of hopeless addicts together.'

'A sad case,' she answered, kissing him back at the corners of his mouth as he tried to speak.

His hand came up and pressed against her lips. His voice was intense. Fraught. 'I can't lose you. It's taken me a lifetime to find you, Lulu. I want to be with you. Can you do that? Let me be part of your life?'

She closed her eyes and revelled in the warmth of his sweet embrace, which was so full of love and compassion. He meant it. There was no doubt. He wanted her as much as she wanted him. But did he need her?

'You have such a big heart,' she whispered as her fingertips ran across the muscles of his chest and collarbone to his jawline. 'I know that you mean those words now, at this minute and in this place, but some time soon you are going to take a telephone call, and then I'll be driving you to the airport.'

Kyle sighed and nodded before replying. 'You're right. I've been assigned to Nepal for another month before the winter closes in. Then there is Africa.'

She smiled as she stroked his face. 'I have good reason to know what it feels like to be left behind by the only person you truly care about in the world.'

'What about the person who's leaving their love behind?' He smiled back, his fingers playing with the curls in her hair. 'Do you have any idea how hard it is to smile and wave and know that you are going to miss everything about them? Especially when I have moments like this to re-member.'

Her smile faded. 'Yes. I know that it would hard for both of us.'

She looked at Kyle, and there was so much pain in her eyes that he reached out with both arms and she fell into them.

'My mother broke my heart. And the pain was so terrible that I blamed her for it for a very long time. I never want to feel that way about you, Kyle. That wouldn't be fair on you.'

Kyle cuddled her closer, his hands stroking her back in wide circles. 'It doesn't have to be that way with us.'

He pulled back from her just enough so that she could see one side of his face, illuminated by the sunlight streaming into the room. The sculpted curved lines of his cheeks and jaw had not been created by some Renaissance master but through a hard life of years of work. Shame that it made absolutely no difference to how much she wanted to run her fingers along that skin and feel the man beneath.

With the kind of smile that would have saved her a fortune in central heating, Kyle said, 'Now—it is probably time to get back to work. You have a birthday party to organize, and I have to write the last two chapters of my book. Although I do have one request.'

He grinned down at Lulu as he slowly drew her to her feet. 'Any chance you could dig out that grey suit? As passion killers go, it was a winner. Otherwise there is absolutely no guarantee that I will be able to keep my hands off you.'

# CHAPTER TEN

KYLE glanced around the brightly lit hallway of Taylor House and waved as he was recognised by many of the jovial people in the crowd.

Show tunes from Hollywood musicals were playing in the background, just loud enough to be heard against the laughter and contented chatter of the old friends and neighbours around him. He had helped some of the men from the Feathers string fairy lights along the trees leading up to the porch and hallway, and now at seven in the evening, they looked terrific.

He quickly scanned the hallway and sitting room for Lulu. Then he heard her distinctive laughter echo out from the kitchen and slowly made his way towards the source, acknowledging warm greetings from people he had only met a few days earlier, who had taken the time to make him feel welcome. Part of their community.

Lulu was standing at the makeshift bar spread out on the long pine table, her attention focused on Emma Carmichael, who had taken up residence at one end with her hand firmly clutched around what looked like a champagne bottle. More Christmas lights had been strung around the kitchen windows, but they paled into a dull glow compared to the woman he was looking at.

It could only be Lulu.

Her long, sensitive fingers were stretched out around a wide bottle, pouring golden sparkling liquid into champagne glasses. Her slender wrists jangled and sparkled with rows of gold bracelets. Bright yellow. Some inset with coloured stones.

A pale green and gold top in shining silk fitted her upper body and highlighted her tiny waist, where a band of pale skin was exposed just at the curve of her back. It was only a few inches wide, but it was enough.

Kyle stopped short, trying to record the image.

An elegant green silk sari was wrapped around her body, heavily embroidered with gold flowers and just short enough to reveal thin gold sandals. He could not help but stare at the gold ankle chains decorated with tiny bells that emerged as Lulu stepped forward on the terra cotta tiled flooring to return the champagne to the ice bucket.

Lulu half turned towards Kyle just as he was about to say hello, and he stalled, stunned by the woman he could not drag his eyes away from.

Three heavy gold necklaces of varying lengths hung below her face, drawing his attention to her fitted bodice and the tantalising curves of what lay beneath.

Then her earrings moved, sparkling in the coloured lights, making him focus on her face. Stunning make-up illuminated her blue eyes, which matched the colour of the silk cloth. Her lips were full, moist, her face radiant.

She had never looked more beautiful. Or more magical.

This was the Lulu he remembered working in

her garden the very first time he had come to this house. This was the real Lulu.

The Lulu he had fallen in love with as she sawed wood and played with her dog.

The fact that he had not realised that fact until this moment shocked him so much that he could only stand and stare as she turned and spotted him.

He was in love with Lulu Hamilton. Not Ruth's little girl, but this unique, amazing woman who was grinning at him from across the room.

'Hello, Kyle,' she said, although his brain was telling him that her radiant smile was more than just a simple hello. 'I'm pleased that you could make it. There are lots of people from the hospice team who would love to meet you. The Bennett sisters have even brought their autograph book.'

Her voice, her smiling face. The way her eyes met his without hesitation or excuse. Welcoming. She wanted him to be here, with her.

Kyle swallowed down a lump in his throat. If this was what being in a real home meant, he had been missing out all of his life.

'Wouldn't miss it for the world,' he answered,

well aware that he had a stupid teenage-crush grin plastered all over his face as he walked slowly over to her and inhaled her exotic perfume, half closing his eyes at the intensity of the spicy floral scent. Roses, vanilla, sandalwood. And Lulu.

'That perfume is perfect.'

She tilted her head at him so that he could sniff closer to her neck without the rest of the village calling the police. 'A present from Emma. I'm glad you like it.'

'Have I told you yet that you look…' he breathed in and raised his eyebrows '…totally amazing?' He whispered in her right ear, 'And seriously hot. You should never wear grey again.'

She reared back and stared into his face. 'Seriously?'

He nodded, and silently mouthed the word 'hot' before taking her hand. 'I am now officially on chaperon duty. Because in that outfit you need one.'

Lulu laughed and grabbed his hand. 'How gallant. Oh, and for the record, you don't look too bad yourself. You should wear a dinner jacket more often. Is it one of your dad's?'

She had the great pleasure of seeing Kyle's neck flush red with the truth.

Of course there was no way that she was going to tell him that he looked so gorgeous that she had almost fainted when she saw him strolling like a male model into her kitchen. She might have guessed that Kyle was one of those men who had been born to wear evening dress. The broad shoulders and slim waist were divine.

James Bond did not even come close.

His short hair had been waxed into a shiny mass swept back above a clean-shaven face. The cleft in his broad chin widened as he grinned back at her, revealing the laughter creases around his mouth and at the corners of both eyes. And then there were his eyes. No, she couldn't look into those eyes.

She would drown and not come up for air. And be happy to do it.

She would snatch at this chance to find a little happiness in her life.

To save herself from doing something foolish, like patting his bottom or suggesting they take a tour of the bedrooms, Lulu started walking from group to group, introducing Kyle to those friends and neighbours he was on nodding acquaintance with from the Feathers and his walks.

'Of course there is one thing I haven't tried yet,' Kyle said between half-closed lips, as his hand moved down to wrap itself around the bare skin at Lulu's waist, his fingers lingering just a second too long before moving to her silk skirt as he drew her into the living room.

He turned and looked into her eyes with that special look for the first time that evening. And her heart melted. The intensity, the need, the loneliness were all there.

In that one single look.

'Dancing,' he whispered into her ear, 'is the only way a poor bloke like me can move closer to a lady without getting his face slapped.'

'Oh, don't be so sure of that,' Lulu said. 'The night is still young.' And with a beaming smile, she raised her left hand to his shoulder.

In seconds his hand was splayed out on her bare waist, pulling her to his body as the music changed to a big orchestra sound.

'Ready to strut your funky stuff?' he asked.
'With a poor wounded medic? I shall try not to step
on your dainty toes. Are you willing to risk it?'

Lulu looked into his grinning face.

Daring to risk it, more like! Daring to be pressed
against his chest. With her flat sandals she only
came up to his chin. How ridiculous was that?
How amazing. How…wonderful.

A second later and Kyle had swept her into
the room, and he had yet another skill at which
he excelled.

'Not bad. Not bad at all,' Lulu reported, as they
completed a tour of the room in harmony with the
music and each other.

To her eternal embarrassment, at that precise
moment she looked over Kyle's shoulder just in
time to see Emma staring at them. If that was not
bad enough, Emma gave her a knowing nod as she
raised one thumb. With a wink. As subtle as ever.

Well aware that her face was warming the
room, as well as her neck, Lulu leant forward
to get out of eyeshot and found herself peering
into Kyle's black bow tie, sensing the mascu-

linity of the man who was holding her in his arms. *Oh, boy.*

'Not too much for you, is it? Want to take a break and catch your breath?'

His hand moved up an inch from the waistband of her silk skirt until it was resting on bare skin, the rough fingertips light and tender. As she looked up into his face the music and chatter in the room faded away, until she felt that they were alone in a private room.

A room dedicated to just the two of them.

Lulu resisted the urge to close her eyes and succumb to the luxury of the moment.

Suddenly she lurched forward as a pair of small arms wrapped around her leg and tried to drag her away to the open French windows.

'Aunty Lulu, Aunty Lulu—Belle ran away, Aunty Lulu. Come quick. Come quick.'

Lulu glanced up at Kyle with a mischievous look before answering. 'It's okay, Pip. Uncle Kyle is going to find her for you. Aren't you, Uncle Kyle?'

Uncle Kyle said something under his breath

about a certain dog that was not suitable for the ears of small persons and released Lulu with a heavy sigh.

Pip immediately grabbed his right hand and dragged him out of the room. Kyle could only manage one half glance back towards Lulu, with a shrug of his shoulders, before he disappeared into the night.

That dog had an agenda. She had thought so before, but now she was sure of it. Lulu stared after Kyle for a few seconds, before the local grocer tapped her on the shoulder and she was off dancing once more.

It was a party.

Why not let her hair down and have some fun for once in her life?

Lulu stood in the front porch of her house and waved as the last of the guests staggered away down the lane towards the village, guided by the lovely fairy lights.

Thank goodness most of them lived within walking distance. Despite the gusting wind, the clear, dry weather had lasted. Unlike her bar. Although nobody seemed to have noticed that she had run out of everything except fruit juice almost an hour ago, when Kyle had taken over from Emma as head barman.

Emma's party was over. And this time next year Lulu would be a student at art school. She would have to rent out the house to pay for it, of course. This truly was the end of an era.

Stars were appearing between the light clouds above the trees as she looked out across the garden. Despite the cold, and her silk sari, Lulu stepped out onto the patio and walked slowly around to the main French windows which led into the living room.

Only to find that she had one guest still in place.

Kyle was stretched out on the sofa by the fireplace. She could just see his face in the glow from the dying fire. Music from Emma's favourite musicals still played softly from the incongruous ghetto blaster borrowed from one of her nephews who worked as a disc jockey at the Feathers, the sound amplified by the silence of the night air so that Lulu could just make out the individual song lyrics.

She stood at the patio door and watched him for a moment. His eyes were closed and his long legs were stretched out over the arm of the sofa, ankles crossed, so that his trousers had ridden up, revealing a tantalising strip of muscular leg above his smart black socks. It would be so very, very tempting to tiptoe across in her sandals and run her fingers up and down that skin and find out if he was ticklish or not.

And then do the same with other areas of his body. Such as the wonderful chest she had seen a few days earlier after his soaking in the river. That was one image had been seared into her brain.

A broad, open-mouthed grin of delight popped across her face as she tried to imagine what her father would have said if he had strolled into this room to find an adrenaline junkie dozing on his sofa. The very thought made her want to giggle, and she pressed her hand across her mouth to stop herself waking Kyle.

Because she wanted this moment to last as long as possible.

She wanted to remember what these little bubbles of happiness felt like when she looked into that tanned stubbly face above those spectacular broad shoulders and… Oh, she would have no problem remembering the touch of his hand on her waist as they danced together. No problem at all.

There went another little bubble of joy.

Making her grin again.

The scar on his upper lip was more pronounced this evening. Dark eyelashes fluttered below heavy eyebrows.

This man had pressed buttons she hadn't known that she even had. He had shown her what being in love could be truly like. She tilted her head so that she could look more closely at the movement of his chest rising and falling.

She was willing to take that risk with this man.

Watching him lying there, his face relaxed, warm, handsome, she knew it would be so easy to be seduced by the sweet and tender kisses of the man she loved.

Tonight had swept away any lingering unspoken doubts she might have had.

This was what she had been frightened of—what she had always feared would happen when she gave her heart. And she *had* truly given her heart. No doubt about it. They had become attached with bonds you could not cut with a sharp tongue or a kitchen knife.

How was she going to walk away from this man? When she wanted him so much? She knew that she was setting herself up for loneliness and pain if she walked down that road.

Kyle stirred slightly and she grinned at him. 'You did a wonderful job with the lights. It was a super idea, Kyle. Thank you for that.'

The hazel eyes remained tight shut as he replied. 'You are most welcome. Remind me not to volunteer to be barman again, would you? Those people can drink.'

There was a sigh from the sofa, and Lulu turned her back to the room and wandered out onto the patio so that he could rest.

In the clear, crisp air, the faint streetlights from

the village gave a background glow as one by one the familiar lights from the farmhouses on the other side of the fields blinked out, leaving the garden dark in the cool breeze that moved the trees.

One of the family of barn owls which roosted in the next copse sounded out, ready to begin its night flight.

There was a faint rustling noise from the room behind her, and Lulu felt soft, warm cloth being draped around her shoulders. Kyle's jacket.

'Is that better?'

Lulu could only manage a nod, and wrapped her arms together across her body to stop the shivers running down her spine.

Only this was not the cold. It was Kyle's body pressed against her back.

She could feel the warmth of his chest through her clothing, and without thinking or hesitating she leant backwards, daring to test the comfort she knew she would find there. His left arm draped around her waist and Kyle rested his head gently on top of hers as he looked out into the garden, then skywards.

'Do you know that the people I work with still follow a calendar controlled by the moon and the stars?' Kyle pointed over to the far right, where a thin silver disc had appeared above the horizon. 'Do you see that new moon? In Nepal it marks the start of a new beginning. A time for festivals. Processions with dancing and singing. It is great fun.'

'You must really miss your life in Nepal. Your patients,' Lulu answered, without moving position.

Kyle hesitated for a moment before answering. 'The people. That's who I miss. The work is the same no matter where I go, whether it is London or Nepal, but the people are special.'

She slowly twisted her body around so that there were only inches between them, so close she could sense the pounding of his heart in tune with her own.

Kyle raised his hand and stroked her cheek with the knuckles, from temple to neck and then back again, forcing her to look into his eyes.

'They love celebrations for a new beginning. A new start. You have chosen a very auspicious day to hold a party for the birthday girl.'

'And what about you? Are you looking for a new start, Kyle? A new beginning?'

Lulu looked up into Kyle's face as he gently stroked hers before replying.

'Maybe I am. Maybe we all are. Would you like to have one last dance to celebrate, pretty girl?' He pressed her fingers to his lips, his eyes never leaving hers.

Lulu leant into his broad shoulder, cuddling into his warmth, sensing and hearing the pounding of his heart as she slid her own arms around his neck.

She had no need of hearing.

No need of sight.

Just the smell of his body. His own unique aroma.

She closed her eyes and revelled in the sensation of his hand on the bare skin at her waist, pressing her even closer to his chest as he moved to the music, his hard-muscled body swaying to the beat.

Her head moved closer, so that she could touch her face against his. Content.

She sensed his arm moving away, then slowly,

slowly, he stepped back so that his hand could take hold of hers, their fingers intermeshing.

She opened her eyes to focus on the man so close, so very close to her body. And felt the power of that rush of heat. Kyle was breathing heavily, its pace matching her own, his eyes darting all over her face.

It was Lulu who had the courage to say the words. 'Can you stay a little longer?'

His reply was a long exhale, followed by a hoarse whisper. 'I'm not going anywhere tonight. But there is something I need to tell you. It can't wait until morning.'

His hands closed around her cool, slender fingers and he led her slowly back into the dining room, the warmth of his smile hotter than the log fire burning in the grate.

She could only grin back in return as he released her hand so that she could wrap it around his waist and press her head into his shoulder.

'Now you really have me intrigued. What is it? What do you have to tell me?'

Kyle slowly turned her around, so that they

were facing each other, and suddenly Lulu felt the air between them grow cold. The look on his face told her everything she needed to know. This was not going to be good news.

'Please? I would like to know what is going on.'

He nodded. 'I've decided to leave early. I'll be going in the morning.'

Lulu stared out of the French windows, her eyes fixed on the movement of the wind in the trees she could just make out in the light from the house and the drive. The gentle waving of branches to and fro in the breeze was no match to the tornado spinning inside her head.

It felt as though she had been strapped onto a horse on a childhood nightmare of a merry-go-round which had started whirling faster and faster, until all she could do was hang on for dear life, knowing that if she even tried to get off she would be seriously hurt.

Only to be slammed to a crushing stop into a large solid object called life.

He was leaving. Just as her mother had, and then her father. She had always known that this was a temporary arrangement. A few weeks out of her life. It wasn't meant to be so hard to say goodbye. She just wanted him to stay so badly.

Kyle snuggled next to her in silence, so that the left side of his body was pressed against her right. Leg to leg, hip to hip, arm to arm. Her body instinctively yearned to lean closer, so that her head could rest against that broad shoulder, but she fought the delicious sensation.

She had to.

It was almost a physical pain when the fingers of his left hand started to slowly unclench the fist she had not even realised was there. Slowly, slowly, she looked up into the most amazing hazel eyes she had ever seen. The dark flecks of cinnamon and forest-green seemed warmer tonight, in the soft light, but in that moment she could see there was something more. Something she had never seen before. Something different. His unsmiling eyes scanned her face for a few minutes, as though searching for an answer to some unasked question he had not the words to speak.

Uncertainty. Concern. Regret, even.

It was all there in the hard lines of his remarkable face, the shadows and planes highlighted by
the flickering firelight. His fingertips clenched
around hers just tight enough to draw her attention away from his darkening eyes—only their
bodies were so close that she could feel the beat
of his heart through the thin fabric of his shirt
against her blouse. Her breathing seemed to
increase, to match the pace of his, and as she
looked up his lips parted so he could take in a
deep, shuddering breath.

Was it possible that Kyle was hurting as much
as she was?

The voice that came from his lips was low,
harsh and barely above a whisper. Trembling.
Uncertain. 'There is one final request. I would
like you to read the last few pages of my diary
before I leave.'

His right hand came up and gently lifted a coil of
her hair behind her ear in a gesture so tender and
loving that she closed her eyes in the pleasure of it.

'It's not going to be easy for you. For one thing
the handwriting is even worse than usual, but I do

have a feeble excuse.' The sides of his mouth
twisted for a second, but there was no laughter.
'I wrote them in the back of the ancient truck
sent to evacuate us from the clinic. It was the first
time I'd had a chance to sit down for days, and
somehow it seemed right to—well, to try and
make some sense of the mess we were in after
Ruth's death.'

His fingers started teasing out individual coils
of hair, as though that was the most important
thing in the world to do at that moment.

Lulu's heart fluttered. This was it. There was
some terrible truth about her mother's death
and he didn't know how to tell her. He was
trying to be gentle.

She tried desperately to remind herself of all of
the terrible options she had imagined and dreamt
up over the years. Surely nothing he could tell her
now would come close to the horror of those
nightmares?

Lulu clasped her fingers around his.

'Kyle? Are you telling me that you saw her at
the clinic on the day she was killed?'

He nodded, once, and then his head dropped for a second before he looked up and stared directly into her startled blue eyes.

'I was probably the last person to see her alive.'

# CHAPTER ELEVEN

'THEN I don't want to read what happened in the pages of your diary or this new book. I want you to tell me in person. Now. To my face. What happened, Kyle? You are the only one who can tell me the truth. Can you do that?'

The powerful legs shifted, and he released her to run his fingers through his hair and walk slowly back to the table spread with papers. He slowly reached out and lifted up the photograph of her mother standing with the local children. One finger traced across the image in silence.

'It had been a hard couple of weeks. We were all exhausted.'

He lowered the photograph to the table and rested his hands, palms down, on the flat surface.

But he turned slightly, so that there was no doubt that Lulu could hear precisely what he was saying.

'Ruth had promised the local chiefs that we would get to the village medical stations once a week. So we'd agreed a timetable. No matter what happened, I would go out in the ambulance every Tuesday morning and Ruth would stay at the hospital.'

After one sideways glance at her, he focused back on the photograph and gave a small shrug.

'You know what she was like—once she had made a promise there was no compromise. It actually seemed to work for a couple of months, but then the fighting started to get closer, and fresh casualties were coming in almost every day. Every bed in the clinic was taken and we had patients in corridors. It was relentless.'

He paused and suddenly found something quite fascinating to look at on the table.

'Go on,' she whispered under her breath. 'It was relentless and you were all exhausted?'

'Lulu, I...'

With one smooth movement, she took a few

faltering steps closer, so that she could press the palms of both hands flat against his chest. The fast, hard beating of the heart that lay beneath told her everything she needed to know.

'It's okay,' she murmured, her eyes locked onto his. 'You can do this. I know you can. Just close your eyes and say the words and it will be over. I'm not afraid. I trust you.'

A shuddering long breath blew across her skin, and her eyes scanned his face in concern until his shoulders relaxed a little.

'It was a nightmare. You know how green I was. They don't teach you how to deal with situations like that in medical school. They can't. The wounded were being carried in by their families on carts and donkeys. All day and then all night. It seemed never-ending. The paramedics did amazing work, but Ruth and I were the only two surgeons, so we both had to work flat out, taking turns to catch a few hours' sleep whenever we could.'

He raised one hand and slid his fingers through her hair until he found the base of her neck. Drawing her closer, he lowered his forehead to hers so that each hot breath fanned her face with its intensity.

'The fighting was getting closer, and we had been working thirty-six hours non-stop. I came out of surgery just before dawn, and Ruth insisted I get some sleep before I dropped.'

He paused and raised his head away from her, to look at the ceiling. When he lowered it to look at her there were tears glinting in the corners.

'I came out of my tent just in time to see Ruth jump into our rackety old ambulance. I shouted out for her to wait for me, but she just gave me a wave and took off down the track in a cloud of red dust.' His voice faltered, and the Adam's apple in his throat twisted hard as he swallowed down the tears and the grief that threatened to engulf them both. 'It was the last time I saw her.'

'Oh, Kyle.' The words closed her throat, and she dropped her head to the comfort and safety and warmth of his broad chest, unable speak.

How long they stayed like that she didn't know, but it was Kyle who broke the silence, his lips pressed into her hair as he spoke.

'Don't feel sorry for me, Lulu. I am not telling you what happened because I want you to feel sorry for me. *You* are the one who deserves sympathy. You and your father were the ones she left behind. If only she had waited a few more minutes. You have no idea how guilty I feel every time I think about it.'

A cold shiver seemed to wave across Lulu's shoulders.

'Guilty? Why should you feel guilty? What difference would a few minutes have made? She was doing the work she loved.'

Kyle's hand pressed harder to the back of her head, as though getting ready to cushion her from the blow to come.

'You don't understand, Lulu. It was a *Tuesday* morning. *I* should have been the one in that ambulance. Not your mother. *I* should have been the one who was killed that day.'

Lulu pushed away from Kyle and staggered towards the table.

'Lulu? Talk to me. Let me explain.'

She held up one hand as she forced air down into

her frozen lungs, a maelstrom of emotions welling up inside her chest and threatening to explode.

'*It was a Tuesday*. It was *your* turn to go out in the ambulance. Is that what you are telling me?'

The voice that came out of her mouth sounded like that of another woman. A woman who had just flung open the doors behind which every nightmare she had ever had were stored and hidden.

'Yes. It was my turn. Ruth told the nurse not to wake me and she took my place that day. Oh, Lulu, I am so sorry.'

Kyle reached out to take Lulu's hands, but she lifted them up and away from him.

'Don't do this, Lulu. Give me your worst— because nothing could be as bad as the guilt I feel every time I even think about that morning. Have you any idea how many times I have asked myself, *What if?* What if I hadn't been so exhausted and fallen asleep that morning? What if Ruth had waited another ten minutes? Or not been so stubborn? Or here's a good one. What if we had called the army to check whether they knew about the landmines on that road?'

'Stop. Stop it, Kyle. I don't want to hear any more.' Lulu wrapped her arms around her body to try and control the violent shivering. 'Is that the real reason why you are here right now? Why you agreed to write this book when it is obviously the very last thing that you want to do? It is, isn't it? You feel that you have to make amends for dodging a land mine? Was that how Mike black-mailed you to come here? By using your guilt that you survived?'

'Far from it. You see, Mike doesn't know that it should have been me who died that day. You are the only person I have ever told. The only person I ever would tell.'

'Me?' She stared at him for a few seconds, wide-eyed, before nodding her head.

'Of course. I see it now. That is why you agreed to come to this house instead of working in London. You are trying to compensate for your own guilt by being nice to me. Taking care of me. Is that it, Kyle? You think that you have some ob-ligation to look out for me because you survived and she didn't?'

She was shouting now and she didn't care. Fists clenched, she strode up to him and stared into his shocked and pale face.

'How much do you like *me*? Or are you only interested in Ruth Taylor Hamilton's daughter? Please—I'd like to know the answer to that question before I throw you out.'

'So what if I do feel obligated?' Kyle snatched up the photograph of her mother laughing under the hot African sun. 'I owe her my life and I had no idea that she had a child. What is so wrong with my wanting to make sure that you have everything you need?'

He moved forward to clasp hold of both of her forearms, only she stepped away and crossed her arms tight, blocking any contact at all.

'But that was two weeks ago. Since then everything has changed. I had no way of knowing how much I would come to care about you. Want to be with you. And, no, *not* as Ruth's little girl. You are an amazing woman in your own right, Lulu Hamilton. You have to know that. Ruth would have been so proud.'

'Thank you for answering my question,' Lulu replied in a calmer voice, her eyes fixed on something fascinating on the carpet. 'But she's gone. And there is not one thing either of us can do to bring her back.'

She slowly raised her head and locked eyes with Kyle through her blurred tears.

'She took the decision to leave you behind that day—just as she took the decision to leave me behind every time she walked out of the door en route to some airport—any airport.' Lulu raised one hand. 'That was her choice. She was head of the clinic and she had a job to do. It was her decision to go out that day. Not yours. And certainly not mine.' She shook her head before stepping back. 'I've had to live with those decisions all my life. Now it's your turn. So if that is the reason you are here, you can consider yourself officially off the hook. Duty done.'

'What are you saying?'

'My part in this project is over. I've done everything I promised.' She waved one hand towards the boxes of paperwork. 'You can have the diaries and letters. Whatever you want. Just take them and go back to Nepal, or wherever it is you have to go back to so urgently. And allow me to get back to my life.'

'Lulu—please. Let's talk this through. I don't want to leave you like this.'

She looked hard at Kyle, lifted her head, and spoke in a clear, distinct voice.

'I don't want to talk about it. I want you to leave now. Please close the door behind you on the way out.'

And with that, she turned her back on him and walked with as much control as she could to the French windows. It was only when the curtains were almost closed that she saw the headlights of his car swing out of the drive and head off down the lane.

Dropping her hands away from the cords, she collapsed down on the window seat and put her head in her hands, let the shock take over. How long she sat there sobbing she did not know, but the air grew cold around her and she did not care.

Slowly, she became aware that a red-brown

shape was standing patiently by her side, and as she sat up Belle gently laid her head on Lulu's lap and sat quietly, her deep brown eyes looking up at her. She wrapped her arms around the dog's head and let the tears stream down her face and into the dog's fur.

'Looks like it's back to just you and me, Belle. On our own again. Just you and me.'

Early the next morning over a half-hearted breakfast, Emma rubbed Lulu's shoulder as she dropped her head onto her outstretched arms.

'You knew it was going to be hard. But you can do this.' She dragged Lulu to her feet. 'Right? Right. Come on, girl, I'll make the coffee and you get back to work. Those paintings won't paint themselves. It will help.'

Lulu shrugged an ancient sweater over her overalls. Emma was right. She needed to work on something—anything—to focus her mind and control the turmoil that raged inside her.

She had to get back to her old life.

The past two weeks working with Kyle had been

a disaster for her painting projects. The gallery had already called to find out how many watercolours of local wild flowers she could provide. They were always in demand as Christmas gifts and hand-painted greeting cards—she was going to have to work fast if she had any chance of making the Christmas deadline now that the book project was behind her.

Over and done with.

Finished.

*I don't want it to be over,* she thought. *I don't want to be without him in my life*. But she dared not form those words. She had tasted something so wonderful it was hard to imagine life without that flavour again.

How could she have fallen so deeply, so fast?

In another world they might even have had a chance to make a life together. She knew what his world was like without any complicated excuses. They understood one another without having to explain.

Except, of course, he had not been honest with her.

Lulu dropped her shoulders and closed her eyes tight shut for a moment, before slowly twisting around in her chair to look at her mother's portrait.

This was where her father had sat, day after day. Joined for ever to the woman who still had the power to control their lives.

Ten years ago that woman had decided to let her exhausted new surgeon sleep after working through an African night. One single decision, made for the best of reasons. And Kyle had been punishing himself ever since.

'Oh, Mum,' she whispered. 'Look what you did. You gave me someone to love. Thank you for that. Any chance you can find a way to get him back for me?'

With a fast shiver, and a shake of her head for being so ridiculous as to talk to a painting, Lulu turned back to her work and wiped away the salty tears from her eyes.

Her painting was her refuge. Her solace.

And she had never needed that solace more than today.

She quickly pulled out her portfolio and lifted

the first drawing onto the table in front of the window. A cluster of spring primroses peeked out from wide, fleshy leaves. It was a pretty still-life, in delicate shades of pale yellow and green that would sell well. There was nothing daring or brave or exciting about it, but it was true to life and simple. Natural and attractive.

Except that as she examined it more closely under natural daylight she saw that the original pencil drawing was too dark for the pale watercolours she had used, not daring to be too bold, and the leaves were out of proportion with the flowers.

The whole symmetry of the piece seemed wrong to her now.

It would take hours of work with layers of paint and tiny brushes to correct the mistakes and give the painting shadow, depth and texture. To make it come alive.

Suddenly the whole piece looked flat, boring, dull and mediocre.

Where was the life? The wonderful rich and vibrant colour and texture she thought she had created? How had she failed so miserably?

No one would notice the flaws from a distance. The actual painting was no bigger than a hardback book, with a huge white border that would be hidden beneath the mount and the picture frame. But *she* knew they were there.

What she been satisfied to accept a few days earlier was no longer good enough.

Which was why Lulu grabbed the top edge of the sheet of heavy paper with both hands and ripped it down the middle with all of the strength in her body, then again and again, until the table was littered with torn fragments of white and coloured paper.

Heart thumping, she stared down at the pieces with a smile on her face as a sense of freedom pulsed through her. *Liberated.*

She didn't want to go to art college and paint botanical drawings—she could already do that. She was going to art college to find out what she was capable of.

In an instant she had swept her watercolour box and portfolio off the table and replaced it with her father's large sketchpad. Twice the size of her own. Well used. And just what she needed.

Lulu could only smile as she flicked through the old sketchpad she remembered from being a girl. The spine was almost broken, and as she flicked to the next clean page a loose piece of paper fluttered out.

Swooping it up, she suddenly took a sharp intake of breath. This was not a sketch or a drawing, but a single sheet of familiar thin airmail paper covered in pale blue ink.

It was her mother's writing.

Her legs threatened to give way and Lulu collapsed at the table. She certainly had not seen this letter before.

She turned the sheet over in her hands. It looked like a page from one of her mum's letters, except their address had been scribbled on the reverse. That was unusual; she'd usually tried to fill both sides of the pages with tiny thin letters, so she could cram as much as possible into the mailing.

Not this time.

The writing was thin and wobbly, disordered, but with a sense of energy and urgency Lulu did not recognise. There was no date or address to indicate where or when it had been written.

Taking a breath, she read through the words, and then read them again.

*There are only the four of us left now. We have already moved three times during the night, carrying patients and whatever we could save to higher ground, but they are moving faster than we can. The villagers have fled into the hills.*

*We're all too exhausted to go any further, so we sit here waiting for the inevitable. Too tired to talk.*

*I wonder what you are doing in Kingsmede? Working in the garden, perhaps, with Lulu by your side? Or filling the world with colour and light in the happy home I left behind? It must be so pretty now that summer is here.*

*You told me once that our lives are our greatest treasure, our most precious possession. Far too precious to waste on anything which is not capable of breaking our hearts.*

*How very right you were. As always. I am looking at the photograph you sent me from our little girl's last birthday party and my heart is breaking.*

*It is too painful, and the crew are looking for me to get them out of this.*

*I think you are the only person in this world who knows that I could not even try to do what I do, in these hard places, without the knowledge that you are both safe back home.*

*You are my heart. My foundation. Without my family I would not have the strength to get up every day, to work to make things better for these people, knowing that I will probably fail. You are the ones who make this possible for me. And I know you pay the price.*

*At the clinic someone had left behind a book of poetry. I wrote down one of the lines: 'If you love somebody, let them go, for if they return, they were always yours. And if they don't, they never were'.*

*You are strong enough to let me go. Time and time again.*

*I'm going to leave this note in my medical bag. If anything happens to me, someone might post it. Kiss our little girl for me. I love you both. Never forget that.*

There was no signature. No familiar kisses at the bottom. Only a faint mark of the pen as though she had started to write something and been interrupted.

Along the margin, next to the quotation, her dad had written in pencil, 'Quote from Khalil Gibran.'

Lulu slid back against her chair and let the tears flow down her cheeks.

Terrified, Ruth Taylor Hamilton had held this very piece of paper in her own sweaty hand. She had wanted them to know what she was thinking while she waited for the local militia to arrive and execute her, with the crew and the patients.

Was that why her father had taken it from the box of letters and tucked it between the pages of the sketchbook that had never left his side? To remind himself of that great love? A love which was worth breaking his heart over? A love worth that huge risk?

No. *More than that.*

Lulu closed her eyes and inhaled deeply.

Her father had sacrificed his own happiness to make sure that her mother had a stable base to come home to.

He had let her mother go time and time again in the hope that she would return to him.

Knowing that they belonged together.

Knowing that their love was capable of breaking their hearts.

Her father had stayed married to her because that was what her mother had needed. No matter the cost.

'Lulu? What is it?' Emma had come in and was staring down at her, her face anxious and caring. 'What's happened, little girl?'

'She spent so much time away on missions and he was so lonely,' Lulu gulped. 'I always thought that he regretted marrying someone who didn't want to be with us. But I was wrong. I simply never saw it before today.'

Lulu stared down at the page between her fingers, blinking away tears so that she could focus on the faint blue words written so many years ago.

'I've been such a fool. He loved her so much he was willing to let her go. Even if she broke his heart. Their love was so precious. I can see that now.'

'Well, of course it was. They were two sides of the same coin.'

Emma stood back and turned to one side, to gaze up at the portrait of Ruth Taylor Hamilton over the mantel.

'You only have to look at this painting to know how he felt about her. Your father was a clever man, Lulu, and he did love your mother—very much. He knew that Ruth would never be happy with a nine-to-five job in Kingsmede. And he was willing to make the sacrifice so that she could be happy. Every single time she stepped out of that door it broke his heart. But their love kept him going when they were apart. Kept them both going. Because I know that she felt the same way about him. They adored each other.'

Emma looked back with her head tilted and smiled.

'Why am I getting the feeling that this is not just about your parents? Am I right?'

Lulu suddenly sat up straight, blinking away her tears as she stared out of the window into the brightening sky.

'I'm in love with Kyle Munroe and I don't want to lose him. I need him so much, but I know now that I have to let him go. Even if he does break my heart.'

Emma sucked in a sharp breath of air, then grasped Lulu by both arms.

'Then go and tell him how you feel. Or regret it for the rest of your life. Go. As fast as your legs can carry you. I'll lock up here and follow you with Belle. Go! Scoot! You might just be able to catch him in time.'

# CHAPTER TWELVE

*PLEASE let him still be here. Please.* He could not have left yet, could he?

She pedalled faster, and the arms of her old painting overalls puffed out in the cold wind which lifted the chestnut leaves up into loose whirls either side of the lane.

Lulu's heart soared as she saw a flash of dark green in the car park next to the Feathers. *His car was here!*

In one swift movement she swung her legs from her old cycle and leant it against the nearest tree, before running into the reception area, her eyes scanning for Kyle in the lunchtime crowd.

It took Lulu three seconds to bounce up the steps to the bedrooms and stand puffing and panting outside the only closed bedroom door. Emma's best guestroom.

Her hand stretched out towards the door handle. And then she snatched it back.

Eyes closed, she blew out a long deep breath, her head suddenly dizzy with doubt as the blood surged in her veins.

What was she doing here? What if he said thanks, but no thanks? This was crazy.

What had her mother said in her letter? If you love somebody, let them go? She loved this man and yet she was going to let him go free to live his life? Away from her? Mad. Yet she knew deep in her heart that it was absolutely the right thing to do.

She was risking her future happiness on a crazy decision to trust her heart instead of her head.

And what if he said yes? On the one hand she could be committing herself to the life of loneliness that her father had endured—or, on the other, to loving a man who had shown her how to love.

She had to do it now. Or never. Perhaps that was why she felt so naked? Exposed?

After ten seconds of agonised waiting, she

straightened her back and prepared to knock—and at the very second she did so there was movement on the other side of the door. The handle turned on its own and cracked open an inch, then wider, braced by a familiar khaki rucksack.

She was stunned into silence as the door opened and her eyes locked onto his. He looked at her with the kind of intensity that seemed to knock the oxygen from her lungs.

Then those eyes smiled, and she took in the full effect of that handsome face. He grinned straight at her with the kind of smile that turned her legs to jelly. No camera could have captured the look on his face at that moment.

She felt as though the air would explode with the electricity in the air between them.

'Hi.' He smiled. 'You look nice. Although you didn't need to dress up to see me off.'

Lulu glanced down at her oldest pair of painting overalls and smiled back at him, desperate to break the tension so that she could put the words together that she needed to say. Wanted to say.

So much had changed.

'Oh, this little old thing?' she managed in half-breaths.

'I was planning to drive up and see you. I've been pretty busy in the last few hours.' He paused. 'Has something happened? Are you okay?' There was so much love and concern in his voice that any doubts Lulu had had about what she had to do next were wiped away.

'I—I found a note from my mother,' she faltered. 'It was inside Dad's old sketchbook. It said that…' Her throat was so choked the words refused to co-operate.

'Hey. Come and sit down.'

He wrapped his arm around her shoulder and shoved the rucksack aside so that he could draw her inside the room, where he lowered her gently on the bed while he sat on the quilt and held her hand.

'Now, talk to me. And take it slow. Tell me what this letter said that was so important you dragged yourself away from your painting to tell me about it.'

'What did it say?' she replied, stroking his hand as her eyes locked onto his, and all the words she had practised on the cycle ride spilled out in a rush. 'It said that I have been a complete fool. I have been so wrong, Kyle. About so many things.'

She reached up and stroked his cheek, her eyes never leaving his.

'I haven't stopped thinking about what you said. And you were right. This is the biggest risk of my life—your life—anyone's life.'

She breathed in, her heart thudding so loudly she suspected that he must hear it from where he was sitting so quietly.

'I know now that I will always love you, Kyle Munroe, and it doesn't matter where you are in the world. And if that means that I have to let you go—to be free to do your work…' She licked her lips. 'Then that is the way it has to be. I want to be with you. Love you. If you still want me to wait for you?'

Kyle sat very still, staring at her, and she bit her lower lip in fear. She might have just made the biggest mistake of her life, but this was the way it had to be.

'I could be away for six or seven months at a

time, you know,' he told her gently, his voice low, sensual and intimate.

'Probably longer. But I am going to let you go and do what you have to do—wherever that is. Because just maybe we can get back together one day. I love you, Kyle, and that is not going to change whether you are in Nepal or Uganda or down the road.'

Kyle did not answer, but slid her fingers from his so that he could caress her face, his eyes scanning from her nose to her roughly tied-back, out-of-control hair.

'You love me but you are willing to let me go and do the work which means so much to me? Is that right?'

She nodded, afraid to trust her voice. 'As long as you are somewhere in this world, loving me, then I shall be complete. My heart will be your beacon home to my love.'

'Then there's only one answer to your question. No. I don't want you to wait for me.'

Her heart caught in her throat, but he pressed one finger on her lips and smiled, breaking the terror.

'You see, I'm not as brave as you are. As soon as I left you this morning I knew that I couldn't leave the woman I have fallen in love with without trying to come up with some options.'

He grinned at her and slid forward, so that both his hands were cupped around her face as tears pricked her eyes.

'I love you way too much to let you go. I need you, Lulu. I need you so much. Nothing else comes close. What would you say if I told you that I will be working out of London for the next twelve months?'

She shuddered out a chuckle of delight and relief. 'I would say, yes, please, and then I would ask how you have managed it.'

'They love what we've done, Lulu. Not me. The two of us. It seems that we make a pretty good team. Mike Baxter wants me to finish the book over the winter, then work with the media company on a series of follow-on books and documentaries. The Nepal mission is going to be fully funded for the next five years, and I have a job managing the missions in Africa and Asia any time I want one.'

Kyle grinned back and took her hands in his, ready and willing to tease out the delicious moment when she heard the surprise he had planned.

'I did insist on one extra condition before they agreed to double their donation to the foundation. I told them that I would only do it if I could bring my fiancée with me to Nepal next May, so that she could paint the rhododendron forests in bloom. She might be at art college, but she'd deserve first-class travel all of the way.'

'Your fiancée…' She breathed out the words, tears pricking her wide eyes, scarcely daring to believe what he was saying.

'You have given me the greatest compliment a man could wish. You've offered me your love and the freedom to live my life. I never imagined I would find a woman who could love me as much as I loved her. I told you last night that I wasn't going anywhere, and I meant it. Not without you.'

Kyle's voice faltered as he pressed his forehead to her flushed brow.

'Last night, when I held you in my arms, I had the unbelievable feeling that I had come home.

That this was where I belonged. I have travelled all over the world, Lulu. I might have kidded myself that it was for work, but the truth is hard to accept. I needed to prove to myself that there was some reason why I survived and Ruth perished. To prove that I could make a difference to people's lives. Just as she had done.'

'Oh, Kyle. It was never your fault. Just as it wasn't mine. I know that now. And you *have* made a difference.' She was stroking the hair back from his forehead now, her fingertips moving through the short curls as she stared into the depths of those stunning eyes.

'I have never felt such an overwhelming sense of homecoming than in these last few weeks I have spent with you. I didn't even realise that I was looking for it. Your heart is my beacon home. Wherever you are is where I want to be. Bring me home, Lulu. Bring me home.' He knelt in front of her as he whispered, in a husky, intimate voice that she had only heard before in her dreams, 'I love you and I want you to be part of my life, Lulu. If you'll have me?'

Lulu looked into a face so full of love that her heart broke.

'Have you? Oh, my sweet darling. How can you ask that after last night? You have to know that I love you. I will love you for the rest of my life. You are the centre of my world.'

She choked with emotion as Kyle stood, then swung her up into the air, whirling her around and around until her feet connected with the bedroom lampshade.

In an instant Kyle had lowered her to the floor and grabbed her hand. She had to skip down the stairs to keep up with him as they ran out together into the faint sunshine, laughing and squealing in joy. Oblivious to the people around them.

Emma Carmichael stepped out of her car just in time to see Kyle grab Lulu behind the knees and throw her over his right shoulder.

Kyle was almost in the middle of the river before she managed to wriggle free, and then, holding hands, they pulled and twirled each other round and round, heads back, laughing and shouting in pleasure, water splashing up around them, before collapsing into each other's arms, their heads pressed together into a passionate kiss.

At that moment Belle leapt out of the backseat of Emma's car and charged into the water to dance and play around the happy couple, barking and scampering in the shallows.

Emma turned to the rest of the village, who had crowded in to look over her shoulder, and shooed them back inside the Feathers.

'Those Taylor girls always end up with the best-looking boys! Now, who's ready for a nice glass of champagne? There is far too much excitement around here.'

# EPILOGUE

KYLE strolled into the spacious art gallery and looked over the heads of the glamorous patrons to catch a glimpse of the only person he needed to see.

And there she was. The centre of attention, chatting away to friends and buyers as though she attended an exhibition of her own paintings every day of the week.

Incredibly beautiful. Confident. Unique.

Looking at her now, it was hard to imagine that only an hour ago he had been fighting to pin back her corkscrew curls to display the African tribal jewellery that had been her wedding gift from their friends in Uganda.

She looked wonderful.

By some sixth sense, at that precise moment she

turned her head towards him and grinned right back across the room. The familiar heat of attraction flashed through his body. He did not want to be apart from the woman he loved for one moment longer than necessary!

Clusters of people were gathered in front of a wall of brilliantly coloured paintings of exotic blooms. Rhododendron bushes in full bloom, magnolia trees and stunning African blossoms shone out from the walls. Glowing and vibrant. Just like the amazing and beautiful woman who had painted them.

He casually wrapped one arm around the waist of her simple aquamarine silk satin shift dress and was rewarded with a tender kiss on the side of his neck as he drew her closer.

'Have I told you this evening that you look stunning, Mrs Munroe?'

'Um… Once or twice. Thank you, anyway—and you clean up pretty well yourself, Dr Munroe.' She reached up and smoothed down the lapel of his black cashmere suit. 'Although I do have a certain preference for khaki green.' Her mouth lifted into a personal smile that still hit him hard.

'Kyle—glad you could make it.' The beaming gallery owner strolled forward to shake his hand. 'Thank you for delaying your plans for a few days. The exhibition has been a huge success, but we couldn't have done it without Lulu being here. When are you flying out this time?'

'We're leaving for Kampala tomorrow, then Delhi,' Kyle replied, and laughed out loud. 'But don't worry. We shouldn't be gone for more than a few weeks. Unless, of course, my wife decides to take off on yet another botanical expedition of her own. In which case—' he threw his hands up and shrugged in defeat '—who knows where we'll end up? There is no holding this girl back.'

Lulu squeezed his arm as she smiled up into his face. 'Well, there have to be some perks for marrying the director of the foundation responsible for all of Africa and Asia! But then we are going home to Kingsmede. Together. To start the most amazing journey of our lives.'

# MILLS & BOON PUBLISH EIGHT LARGE PRINT TITLES A MONTH. THESE ARE THE EIGHT TITLES FOR MAY 2010.

---

## RUTHLESS MAGNATE, CONVENIENT WIFE
Lynne Graham

## THE PRINCE'S CHAMBERMAID
Sharon Kendrick

## THE VIRGIN AND HIS MAJESTY
Robyn Donald

## INNOCENT SECRETARY… ACCIDENTALLY PREGNANT
Carol Marinelli

## THE GIRL FROM HONEYSUCKLE FARM
Jessica Steele

## ONE DANCE WITH THE COWBOY
Donna Alward

## THE DAREDEVIL TYCOON
Barbara McMahon

## HIRED: SASSY ASSISTANT
Nina Harrington

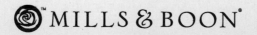

# MILLS & BOON PUBLISH EIGHT LARGE PRINT TITLES A MONTH. THESE ARE THE EIGHT TITLES FOR JUNE 2010.

## THE WEALTHY GREEK'S CONTRACT WIFE
Penny Jordan

## THE INNOCENT'S SURRENDER
Sara Craven

## CASTELLANO'S MISTRESS OF REVENGE
Melanie Milburne

## THE ITALIAN'S ONE-NIGHT LOVE-CHILD
Cathy Williams

## CINDERELLA ON HIS DOORSTEP
Rebecca Winters

## ACCIDENTALLY EXPECTING!
Lucy Gordon

## LIGHTS, CAMERA...KISS THE BOSS
Nikki Logan

## AUSTRALIAN BOSS: DIAMOND RING
Jennie Adams

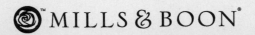